The ~~Jerr~~

MW01138735

~~...~~ _Snapshot)_

## By Sherry A. Burton

Dorry Press

## *Also by Sherry A. Burton*
### *The Orphan Train Saga*
*Discovery (book one)*
*Shameless (book two)*
*Treachery (book three)*
*Guardian (book four)*
*Loyal (book five)*
*Patience (book six)*

### *Orphan Train Extras*
*Ezra's Story*

### *Jerry McNeal Series*
*Always Faithful (book one)*
*Ghostly Guidance (book two)*
*Rambling Spirit (book three)*
*Chosen Path (book four)*
*Port Hope (book five)*
*Cold Case (book six)*
*Wicked Winds (book seven)*
*Mystic Angel (book eight)*
*Uncanny Coincidence (book nine)*
*Chesapeake Chaos (book ten)*
*Village Shenanigans (book eleven)*
*Special Delivery (book twelve)*
*Spirit of Deadwood (a full-length Jerry McNeal novel)*

# The Jerry McNeal Series

## Special Delivery
By Sherry A. Burton

The Jerry McNeal Series: Special Delivery
Copyright 2023

By Sherry A. Burton
Published by Dorry Press
Edited and Formatted by BZHercules.com
Cover by Laura J. Prevost
@laurajprevostphotography
Proofread by Latisha Rich

For more information on the author and her works, please see www.SherryABurton.com

# *Dedication*

I will forever be grateful to my mom, who insisted the dog stay in the series.

To my hubby, thanks for helping me stay in the writing chair.

To my editor, Beth, for allowing me to keep my voice.

To Laura, for EVERYTHING you do to keep me current in both my covers and graphics.

To my beta readers for giving the books an early read.

To my proofreader, Latisha Rich, for the extra set of eyes.

To my fans, for the continued support.

Lastly, to my "writing voices," thank you for all the incredible ideas!

# Chapter One

Jerry McNeal had experienced enough paranormal encounters in his thirty-two years of life that ghostly visits rarely came as a surprise. Still, nothing came remotely close to preparing him for the situation he was currently dealing with.

Jerry lifted the lid to the box and was both relieved and flustered to see soft brown eyes staring out at him. The pup wasn't completely black as Jerry had first thought, as closer inspection showed traces of brown mingled throughout his dark fur. The puppy whined and tried unsuccessfully to climb from the box.

Jerry scowled at the furry beast. "Not a chance, kid. You've kept me up most of the night. The least you can do is keep it down so we don't disturb my parents any more than we already have. Where'd you come from anyway?"

Gunter rose, cocking his head to the side at the sound of the tiny toenails scratching against the cardboard. He moved closer, wagged his tail, and dipped his nose into the box. Jerry smiled as the pup rewarded the ghostly K-9 with eager puppy kisses. That the puppy wasn't afraid of Gunter said a lot. While the law of physics told him his deductions were absolutely ludicrous, that the pup was somehow attached to Gunter was the only explanation for his being there. Jerry recalled Gunter's rendezvous with Lady, the black German shepherd that belonged to Mills, the man living in the camper next to him during his visit to Port Hope. The pup jumped, failed to escape from the box, and sat looking at Jerry while whining his discontent.

Jerry closed his eyes and ran a hand over his head, and the whining stopped. When he opened his eyes, the puppy was gone. Just as he breathed a sigh of relief, he heard a soft growl and looked to see the pup tugging on his pants leg. Jerry resisted a smile. *Don't buy in to it, McNeal. One smile, and the little guy's got you.*

Keeping his face unreadable, Jerry reached down, picked up the pup, and placed him back inside the box. The puppy sat back on his haunches and woofed his disapproval once more.

Jerry glanced at Gunter. "You made him. You entertain him."

Gunter dropped to the floor, placed his muzzle on his paws, and looked up at Jerry as if to say, *You're not going to pin this on me.*

The door opened, and Wayne stepped outside. His father offered him one of the two coffee cups he was holding. "Thought you might need this after the night you had."

Jerry took a sip and nodded. "Sorry, I tried to keep him quiet."

"I didn't hear much. Your mom, on the other hand, said she heard him wailing until around one a.m. Said how she was afraid you smothered him because one minute he was singing the blues and the next nothing. She was going to come to check on you both and then decided she didn't want to know if you snuffed the little guy."

Jerry motioned toward the box. "As you can see, I didn't snuff him. I simply said the heck with it and put him in bed with me. He snuggled right up next to Gunter, and I never heard a peep until about an hour ago when I woke to the sound of him gnawing on Granny's rocker. I have no clue how the little bugger got off the bed without my hearing him. By the way, I need to get you some more paper towels."

Wayne sat and peeked inside the box, which stirred another round of chaos from within. Wayne reached in and petted the pup, instantly settling him. "Have you figured out where he came from yet?"

Jerry looked at Gunter and sighed. "I think it is

safe to assume Gunter brought him."

Wayne nodded. "Lori and I were talking and came to the same conclusion. Does that mean the pup is a ghost?"

Jerry shook his head. "No, if he were a spirit, you wouldn't be able to see him. At least, I don't think so."

"Why's that?"

Jerry watched as the pup chewed on his father's finger. "Because you've never seen a spirit before. Neither has Mom, but you can both see the puppy."

"Gunter's a ghost, and you can see him. From what you say, others can too. What if the puppy's a ghost and wants us to see him?"

Jerry smiled. "Maybe, but I don't think that's the whole of it. Something has the skin on the back of my neck tingling, letting me know there's more to the little guy than meets the eye."

Wayne pulled his finger free and lifted the pup from the box. "He seems solid enough. But since none of us let him in the house, and you're saying he's not a ghost, how do you explain him being here?"

Gunter pushed from the floor and stood, keeping an eye on Wayne and the pup.

Jerry stared at his dad for a few seconds, gathering the courage to answer. Finally, he shrugged. "Danged if I know. Some kind of portal or something. I think he belongs to Gunter."

Wayne raised an eyebrow. "Belongs?"

"I think Gunter might be the father."

The other eyebrow joined the first. Wayne cupped the puppy under the backside and turned him from side to side. The pup didn't appear to mind the scrutinization as he stared back without so much as a twitch. "Is that even possible?"

Jerry looked at Gunter and offered another shrug. "I don't have a clue. All I know is what I saw, and that was Gunter doing the deed with a black shepherd. The owner said the dog was in heat. I know it sounds crazy, Pop, but in my line of work, the square peg sometimes actually fits in the round hole. Things don't add up until they do. And to be honest, it's the only explanation I have right now."

Wayne leaned back in his chair and cradled the pup, scratching it behind the ear. "Okay, son, let's say for the sake of argument that you're right, and Gunter is the father. You're convinced he's not a ghost. Maybe he is a hybrid? If so, can he eat? Sleep? Will he grow? Can he get injured?"

Jerry had to give it to his father – those were all excellent questions – ones that he had been rolling around in his head since the pup appeared the previous day. "I guess 'hybrid' is as good a term as any. And it would explain why the pup appeared out of nowhere. Gunter has been disappearing a lot lately. Maybe he knew about the pup and was going to check on him, which begs the question are there others, or is this guy the only one? As for how the puppy got here, either Gunter purposely brought him here – which I wouldn't put past him – or the pup followed him. Either he likes it here or he's stuck and doesn't know how to get back. He can sleep – I've seen him. It's reasonable to think he can grow – if not, he would still be a newborn, don't you think?"

"Sounds as logical as anything else," Wayne mused.

"Nothing about this sounds logical." Jerry chuckled. "We also know his plumbing works."

Wayne scrunched up his face. "Yeah, about that. Your mother's still sore at us for lying to her about the ghost cat."

Jerry stared at his pop. "Did you tell her it was your idea?"

"Nope, I figured you wouldn't want me to take all the blame." His father grinned and placed the pup back in the box. "Your mom said we need to do more things together. I'm just heeding her words."

The puppy whined and clawed at the box. He jumped up, fell to the bottom, shook off the fall, and made another attempt.

Jerry sighed. "That box isn't going to hold him long. I'm going to have to get him a crate."

Wayne held up a hand. "Your mother's already on it. She was dressed and off before I came outside. Said she was going to go pick up some things for her grandpuppy."

Jerry stared at his father. "You're kidding, right?"

Wayne shook his head. "Her words, not mine." Wayne dipped his hand into his pocket and pulled out a baggie. Opening it, he reached inside and drew out a slice of turkey. Leaning forward, he offered it to the pup, who eagerly accepted the offering. "What's the matter, don't approve of my food choices?" Wayne asked when Jerry sighed.

Jerry ran a hand over his head. "More like I'm glad you offered it. I'm not used to having to feed Gunter. I probably would have ended up letting the puppy starve."

Wayne dumped the contents of the baggie into the box and pocketed the bag. "I reckon that would have solved one of your problems and created yet another."

Both men watched as the puppy devoured the turkey and went to work licking the cardboard box. Jerry eyed his dad. "What other problem?"

"If the puppy dies and becomes a full ghost, he will never grow up. If that happens, you'll never get any sleep nor get the little fellow housebroken."

Jerry smiled and looked at Gunter. Though the dog often went through the motions, he had never actually left a stream – at least not one visible to human eyes.

Wayne laughed and slapped his knee. "Son, I don't even have to ask where your mind just went. I could see it all over your face. I've read enough Stephen King books to tell you that you don't want to go there."

"Yeah, so have I." Jerry sighed. While the thought may have passed through his mind, he would never have gone through with it – even if he wasn't worried about being haunted by the ghost of the puppy. "The question remains, what am I supposed to do with him?"

Wayne's lips curved. "You might want to start by taking it out to the grass."

Jerry glanced into the box to see the pup circling. He scooped the pup from the box and hurried to the yard, placing him in the grass. Sure enough, the moment he sat the puppy down, he squatted and began doing his business.

Wayne went inside and came back a moment later, holding a plastic grocery bag. He opened the door and handed it to Jerry. "You'll need to get a roll of bags to keep with you. Folks around here don't take too kindly to people not cleaning up after their dogs."

Jerry thought about reminding his dad it wasn't his dog, then thought better of it. That the pup was here told him otherwise. He recalled the apartment he'd rented in Pennsylvania and how his landlord, Wells, had left his dog Erma's piles unattended all over the yard. "I never signed up for this," he grumbled as he bent to clean up the puppy's mess.

"Son, I know you might find this laughable, but I guarantee if you were to take a poll, you'd find just about everyone on the planet would gladly change places with you this very moment."

Jerry lifted the bag and looked to the sky. "Okay, I'm ready."

Gunter growled.

At first, Jerry thought the warning was meant for him until he turned and saw the puppy waddling toward the swamp. Jerry raced to the edge of the yard and scooped the puppy into his arms just as he was trotting under the log barrier. The shepherd wiggled and squirmed until he was able to lick the side of Jerry's face. Jerry pulled his head back. "Oh, no you don't. You're not going to wiggle your way into my heart."

The pup yipped.

Gunter stood next to the bag Jerry had dropped when sprinting after the pup. As Jerry bent to pick it up, the K-9 looked at him as if to say, *Yeah, you used to say that about me too.*

# Chapter Two

At a little past eleven, Lori entered through the garage door carrying a small dog crate and several shopping bags. Her face was flushed, and her eyes sparkled as she placed the crate on the floor and poured the remaining items onto the table. "Is my grandpuppy still here? That's what he is, you know."

Jerry raised a brow at the array of toys. "The puppy is still here."

Lori frowned. "He really needs a name."

"I was thinking of calling him Rat since that's what you thought he was," Jerry teased.

"Very funny, Mister. I'm still burning about the whole ghost cat thing. Imagine my own son lying to me like that."

Jerry shot a glance at his dad. Wayne gave him a look that said, *You brought it up. You're on your own this time.* "We," Jerry said, putting emphasis on the word, "are sorry. Dad and I weren't trying to deceive you – not in a bad way. We just didn't have a better explanation at the time and didn't want you freaking out about maybe having rats in the house."

Lori stooped and made kissy sounds, smiling her delight as the puppy boldly trotted over to her. She scooped him up, lifting her chin as he spread puppy kisses over her face. "Aren't you the cutest thing?"

Gunter lowered to his haunches with a grumbling growl as if to say, *What am I? Chopped liver?*

Jerry laughed. "I think your oldest grandson is jealous."

Lori frowned and looked about the room. "Gunter! Oh, my, I completely forgot about him." She stood and rifled through the toys, plucking out a small squeaky Santa mouse. She pressed to squeak the toy, then tossed it across the room. While Gunter ignored the offering, the puppy squirmed to get down. "No, that's not yours. You can have this one." Lori lifted a sturdy rubber football.

Jerry watched as the puppy took it and instantly began chewing. "Something tells me that's not going to last long."

"It's supposed to be chew-proof." She lowered the pup to the floor, and her eyes trailed to the mouse. "It's still there. Doesn't Gunter like it?"

Jerry shrugged. "He's more of a ball boy." At the mention of the word "ball," Gunter lifted his head.

Lori hurried to the table, retrieved a ball, and

tossed it next to the mouse.

The puppy raced past Gunter and retrieved the ball. He started back and saw the mouse. Keeping the ball in his mouth, he attempted to take hold of the mouse. When that didn't work, he dropped the ball, which rolled under the coffee table. The shepherd took hold of the mouse then dropped to the floor, nosing under the coffee table, searching for the wayward ball. Lying on his stomach, staring under the table, the puppy chomped on the mouse, wagging his tail each time it made a noise.

Wayne rose from the chair and pushed the ball toward the puppy, who once again attempted to carry both toys in his mouth at the same time. "Maybe you should call him Greedy," Wayne suggested.

Lori shook her head. "Jerry will do no such thing. He's just a puppy. He'll grow out of that stage. He needs a dignified name."

Jerry had never named anything before but had to admit the thought of doing so rather appealed to him. *Easy, McNeal, sounds like you're actually thinking of keeping him. That's just what you need, another dog. So, what if I am? I've done okay with Gunter.* As the thought came to him, Jerry realized how absurd it was. Gunter was no example – the dog needed nothing from him. On the other hand, the pup would need to be fed, let out, and trained. *You need to figure out your own life before making this kind of commitment.* Jerry sighed.

"Are you okay, Jerry?" Lori asked.

"Yeah, Mom. Just trying to gather the nerve to tell you I'll be leaving soon."

Lori nodded. "I've been expecting it."

"You have?" Jerry was surprised she hadn't put up a fight.

"You never were one to stay in one place too long." She gave him a long look. "I hope someday you will find a place to call home. Perhaps you'll give me some real grandbabies to spoil."

Jerry smiled. "How about we see how things go with the puppy?"

\*\*\*

Gunter lay on the floor near Granny's rocker. The puppy was confined in the crate next to him. While the pup was fast asleep, Gunter watched as Jerry stared at his phone, trying to decide who to call. The easiest way to figure out where the puppy came from would be to contact Jeff Mills and ask if his dog, Lady, had given birth. If Mills said yes, Jerry would then ask if any of them happened to be missing. The next challenge would be explaining to the man why he was asking. The bigger problem was while Jerry had given Mills his number, he had not asked for the man's contact information in return. It would be easy to call April and ask if she had a way to contact the man, especially since it would provide him with an excuse to hear her voice. At the same time, he was reluctant to call her until after he spoke with Holly. While he thought he knew where his heart lay, he needed to be sure before offering false signals. So that left Fred, who probably knew Mills' number by heart. Not that Fred would have a reason to know – it was just that Fred always had the answer for every question presented to him.

*Not this time*. A smile stretched across Jerry's face. *No way Fred would have the number*. Jerry laughed to himself as he searched out Fred's number and pressed dial.

"Jerry, my boy. I was just thinking about you."

"Oh?" Jerry would expect that coming from Granny, Savannah, or Max. People with the gift often knew when someone was thinking about them, but Fred didn't have the gift – at least not that Jerry was aware of.

"Yeah, I was just making myself a note to call you. I thought you'd be happy to know we were able to reach out and get the records updated to show that Doctor Glasco did not kill his wife. We will also place a story in the local paper citing new evidence and expunging the good doctor of any wrongdoing. We could have the team do a couple of social media posts where they are most likely to be seen if you think that would help."

Jerry breathed a sigh of relief, knowing Fred hadn't actually known he was about to call. He shook his head even though he knew the man couldn't see him. "No, I think you've done enough. Crissy seemed content knowing her father didn't kill her mother. If there are any Facebook posts to be made, she can make them after the story goes live."

"Works for me. So, is this a social call or something else?"

"I need a phone number. The guy's name is Jeff Mills. His camper was parked…"

Fred finished his sentence for him. "In the RV lot next to you when you were in Michigan. Hang on. I'll text you his number."

Less than a moment later, Jerry's phone buzzed, showing a message from Fred with the promised number. Jerry couldn't decide if he was disappointed not to have stumped the man or impressed that Fred had gotten him the information so quickly. "I'm beginning to think you weren't kidding when you joked about the chip implant. Seriously, how could you possibly know everything you know?"

Fred chuckled through the phone. "It's my job to know. Listen, don't sound so surprised. I told you before you're one of us now. We take care of family. You stay in a hotel – we know who is in the room next to you. Sometimes, we check out the whole floor. In this case, we needed to know who would be in close proximity to you in case you found yourself in trouble, so we checked out everyone in the RV park."

*Talk about invasion of privacy.* "You don't think that was a bit over the top?"

"McNeal, in our line of work, everything is over the top. What do you need with Mills anyway?"

Jerry had been waiting for this. "You wouldn't believe me if I told you."

"Try me."

"Okay, I think his dog had puppies."

"Yep, dogs do that."

Jerry waited for half a beat to keep the man guessing. "I'm pretty sure Gunter is the father."

From the sound of the coughing on the other end of the phone, Fred had been in the midst of drinking something. Jerry leaned back in his chair and waited for the normally highly composed man to speak. When he did, it was obvious he was choosing his words carefully.

"You're telling me that ghosts can procreate?"

*Be careful how you answer this, McNeal, or you're going to end up in a straitjacket.* Jerry took a calming breath. "Here's what I know. When I was in Michigan, I personally witnessed Gunter connecting with Mills' German shepherd, Lady."

"When you say connecting, you mean…"

"Yes, Fred, that's precisely what I mean. Yesterday, Gunter disappeared and returned with a puppy."

"Is the puppy a ghost?"

"No. All the plumbing works. The pup eats, and

*16*

my parents can see him," Jerry assured him.

"And he just appeared out of thin air?" Fred's voice was filled with wonder.

"Yep."

"And your plan is to call Mills and tell him the puppy is with you?"

"To be perfectly honest, I haven't decided what I plan on telling the man. Mostly, I want to see if he is missing a puppy. If he is, my theory holds water. If not, I'm at a total loss."

"And you're certain no one is trying to pull a fast one?"

"My parents wouldn't do it, and the only other two people who were close were the neighbors, and they'd been gone over an hour before the puppy showed up."

Fred's voice took on a serious tone. "The two that were in the house, that would be Sandy Cottingsworth and Gertrude Martin?"

Jerry stared into the phone. "You know, Fred, at this moment, I don't know whether to be scared or impressed."

"Go for impressed. It will make it easier on all of us," Fred advised.

"There are plenty of other neighbors to choose from. Why pick those two? Are you watching me?"

"We know where you are, but we're not monitoring your every move if that's what you're asking."

"Tell me what I had for breakfast."

"I can't."

Jerry narrowed his eyes. "Can't or won't?"

"The agency is not keeping that close of tabs on you. I assure you it was a lucky guess. We know your parents and who they are most likely to associate with."

Jerry wasn't sure he believed him. But then again, anyone with an electronic device was in danger of being tracked and listened to at any given time.

Fred cut into his thoughts. "Don't tell Mills you have the puppy."

"Is that an order?"

"No, more like strongly advise. If word gets out about the pup, you will never have another private moment. Every reporter on the planet will be after you for your story, and photographers will be hiding in the bushes waiting to get a picture of the pup. You both will be on the cover of every tabloid in the country for the rest of your lives."

"As opposed to having big brother watching my every move."

"Big brother has your best interest at heart," Fred said dryly. "The world can be a hideous place, McNeal. Something like this gets out, and ugly will crawl out of the sewer and give you a reason to use that arsenal you travel with."

"I don't intend on shooting anyone."

"Good intentions go by the wayside when you're trying to protect those you love. You're a smart man, McNeal. We are good, but we can only do so much. If this thing gets out, I can't promise to protect you or those you love. Gunter is safe, as he's virtually untouchable, but the pup – it's better if people around you think he's just a normal dog."

Jerry knew the man was right about keeping the puppy a secret, but not telling Mills he had the pup felt akin to stealing. "It feels dishonest."

"What does?"

"Keeping the puppy without paying the man. Maybe I can send him a check."

Fred laughed. "And say what? Even if you send him something anonymous, he's most likely to think it a scam and tear it up."

"You're not helping."

"You want me to help? I'll help. I'll see he gets a small inheritance from a long-lost uncle. Would that ease your conscience?"

"Because no one would think that's a scam. How much are we talking?"

"Heck, I don't know. What do German shepherds go for these days? Fifteen hundred to two grand?"

Jerry looked at the pup, who'd woken from his nap and was now sitting outside the closed crate. "This pup is special."

"Three thousand. That's my final offer."

"And you'll make it look legit?" Jerry asked, placing the pup back inside the crate and closing the door.

Fred sighed into the phone. "I'll deliver it myself if that makes you feel better."

"I don't think we have to go that far."

"Good, because there's a massive snowstorm making its way across the country. Michigan is the last place I want to be."

At the mention of the snowstorm, Jerry thought of Holly, then instantly, his thoughts turned to April and Max. "I'm going to be heading out later today."

"Where are you heading?"

Jerry sighed into the phone. *Good question.* "I have some business to attend to over in Destin."

"This business, does it have anything to do with that photographer?"

Jerry ran a hand over his head. "Fred, I think it's time we start setting some boundaries when it comes to my personal life."

"If it makes any difference, Barney and I are team April."

Gunter lifted his head and looked in Jerry's direction as if to say, *Me too.*

Jerry sighed. "About those boundaries I was talking about."

"Consider us backed off. How about we talk about something you do want to hear?"

"Like?"

"Like your truck is ready."

"I wouldn't mind talking about that. Where is it, and how do I get it?"

"Where do you want it to be?"

Jerry smiled. "In my parents' driveway."

Fred's laughter floated through the phone. "If you want to stay put a few days, I'm sure that could be arranged."

"And if I don't want to hang around?"

"I can have it waiting at any airport or military base."

"Let me see how my meeting goes, and I'll let you know." Jerry felt a tug on his shoe as he ended the call. He looked down, surprised to see the puppy pulling on his shoestring. He bent and scooped him into his arms and looked at the crate, which was still firmly closed. "A regular little Houdini, aren't you?"

The pup barked.

"What? You like that name?"

The pup answered with another bark.

Jerry thought about his discussion with the trainer and recalled what Mike had said when he first told him about Gunter. *Give the dog time, and it will name itself.* He smiled. "Okay, little man. Houdini it is."

# Chapter Three

Wayne walked into the room, eyed Jerry's bags, and started to reach for one.

"Hang on a minute, Dad."

"If you're thinking about asking me to keep the pup, the answer is no. Your mother has already asked."

Jerry rocked back on his heels. "I hadn't thought about it, but now that you mention it, Mom does seem to like the little guy."

"Yes, and she also likes her social life. Trust me when I say the last thing your mother and I need is a puppy that needs to be trained and housebroken. I need you to promise me that you won't join forces with your mother and try to gang up on me on this."

Jerry smiled. "Don't worry, Pop. I don't think Houdini is the right fit for you."

"That the name you're going with?"

"I think it's only fitting since he just showed up." While Jerry didn't like keeping things from his parents, he'd taken Fred's words to heart and decided against telling them about the pup slipping through the bars of the crate. "Dad, I need to ask you to do something for me."

"Sure, son. What is it?"

"Don't tell anyone where the puppy came from."

"It's kind of hard to tell what I don't know."

Jerry drew in a breath and tried to sound calm. "You told your friends about Gunter."

"Ah, I see where you're going with this. Yes, I told, but I learned my lesson with that. I didn't think adults would act that way."

"You never know how people will react to things that scare them."

"You think they were afraid?"

"Maybe. What some might think is cool, others might think comes from a dark place. You and I know better, but others might not."

Wayne looked him in the eye. "Where do you think the puppy came from? I mean really came from, and how did he get here?"

Jerry worked to keep his face unreadable. "I think Gunter wanted a friend. He found a puppy and brought him here."

"You don't think he's the father?"

*I'd put money on it.* "Naw, that was just me talking nonsense. We both know that's impossible."

Jerry almost recanted when he saw the look of disappointment on his father's face. "Hey, Dad, I was wondering if I could ask another favor?"

"Go on."

"I wanted to know if I can leave my gun bag here."

"You don't think you'll need it?"

Jerry smiled. "I have my pistol. Besides, I know where to find it if I need it."

"Your mother will be happy about your leaving it here."

"Oh yeah? Why is that?"

"It will give her hope that you'll come visit again."

Jerry chuckled. "Neither of you has to worry about that. I promise not to go so long between visits. Either I'll visit you or you can come see me. Either way, we will make sure it happens."

Wayne started to reach for Jerry's sea bag and hesitated. "I'm glad you came, son."

Jerry reached in for an embrace, sighing as his father clapped him on the back several times. "So am I, Pop. So am I. I think my ribs are good enough to handle the bag."

Wayne waved him off and lifted the bag easily to his shoulder. "I've got the easy job. You still have to say goodbye to your mother and pry that puppy from her hands."

"She's not going to cry, is she?"

Wayne laughed a hearty laugh. "Son, you can wager on it. Why, I'd put odds on her having already started. She's probably using the puppy's paw to sop up her tears."

Jerry rolled his neck. "Thanks for the visual, Pop."

"Just preparing you for what's waiting for you on the other side of that door, son."

Jerry followed his dad from the room and stopped at seeing his mother standing there with the dog crate in her hand. The puppy was inside and showed no sign of wanting to escape. She pushed the crate into his hands. "Take this little varmint with you."

Jerry looked at Gunter and then looked in the crate. "Did Houdini do something to upset you?"

"You mean besides peeing on my new Persian rug and chewing the heel off of my good shoes?"

Jerry wrinkled his brow. "How much do I owe you?"

"No, it's my fault. I should have been watching him. Just promise me when you bring him back, he will have better manners."

Jerry looked into the crate. "I'll do my best."

Lori glanced around the room. "Where is Gunter?"

Jerry nodded to the dog, who stood right next to her.

Lori stooped and faced where she thought him to

be standing and spoke. "You, sir, have impeccable manners and are welcome back anytime." She stood and looked at Jerry. While her lip quivered, her eyes were dry. "The same goes for you, son. Promise you won't stay away so long."

"I promise." Jerry set the crate on the floor and stood, gathering his mother in his arms. He felt her shake and knew she was crying. He continued holding her until she pulled away.

Lori wiped at her eyes. She sniffed, and her eyes widened as she nodded toward the crate. Jerry looked to see Houdini halfway through the gate that held it shut. He bent and pushed the pup back inside. The door to the garage opened. Jerry glanced at his mom and lifted a finger to his lips.

Lori nodded her understanding as Wayne came back into the room. "You're going to have your hands full with that one, son."

Wayne stepped up to her side. "Problem with the puppy?"

Lori sighed an exaggerated sigh. "The little stinker ate the heel of my new shoe." She looked at Jerry and winked.

"I guess we should go before he eats anything else." Jerry scooped up the crate, keeping his hand in front, hoping that would stop the puppy from sticking his head out. Once outside, Gunter leapt through the closed door, claiming his spot in the front seat. Jerry smiled and peeked inside the crate.

"Your old man may be glad you're here, but he's not ready to give up his seat."

Jerry opened the back door and placed the crate inside, wondering how long it would take for the pup to escape. He didn't have to wonder for long, as the pup was sitting in the middle of the cargo hold by the time Jerry finished saying his goodbyes and climbed behind the wheel. Jerry glanced at Gunter. "Get in the back."

Gunter tilted his head.

"Don't look at me like that – you're the one who brought him. Either take him back to where you found him or get back there and make sure he doesn't eat anything."

Gunter disappeared. Jerry heard excited whines and looked over his shoulder to see Houdini smothering Gunter with puppy kisses. While the ghostly K-9 emitted a low growl, his smile let Jerry know he was very much enjoying the attention. After a moment, Gunter curled into a ball, and Houdini snuggled next to him.

***

The closer Jerry got to Miramar Beach, the more unsettled he became. As he traveled on US 331 South toward Scenic Gulf Drive, Jerry wondered what he would find when he reached his destination.

Granny's voice mingled with his thoughts. *What do you want to find?*

Jerry looked to the passenger seat and then

checked the rearview mirror. "If you're going to snoop inside my head, you might as well show yourself."

"What kind of way is that to speak to your grandmother?" Laughter filled the car as Granny materialized in the front passenger seat. "I was hoping you'd just think I was a figment of your imagination."

Gunter barked a greeting as a puppyish growl had Granny turning in her seat. "Well, hello there. Who's your friend, Jerry?"

The growl was replaced by a high-pitched bark. Jerry glanced over his shoulder in time to see Gunter paw at the pup's head to silence him. He glanced at his grandmother. "You're telling me you didn't know about this?"

Granny cocked her head. "This?"

"The puppy belongs to Gunter," Jerry said, glancing in the mirror.

"Gunter found himself a puppy?"

Jerry shook his head. "Gunter is the father."

Granny laughed once more. "You know that's impossible, right?"

Jerry tried to gauge her sincerity. "You really don't know?" Jerry drummed his fingers on the steering wheel, then slowed the car and pulled to the side of the freeway. He waited for traffic to clear and got out. Rounding the small car, he opened the back door, put Houdini into the crate, and secured the door.

"What was that all about?" Granny asked when he returned to the driver's seat.

Jerry waited for an opening and then pulled back on the highway. "Just keep an eye on the puppy."

A moment later, Granny gasped and smacked her knee. "Well, would you look at that? He's a ghost."

"Half. Gunter's the father," Jerry clarified.

"How can you be so sure?"

"Because it's the only thing that fits. I saw Gunter making time with a female shepherd. Then a few days ago, he shows up with this puppy, which nearly scared Mom to death."

Granny reached into the back seat and scooped up the puppy. Houdini lifted his lips and snarled. Granny placed a finger under the puppy's muzzle and lifted it so she could look him in the eye. "Cut that out; you're one of us."

"Half," Jerry repeated. "Good to see he will alert when a spirit shows up."

"Spirit smirit," she said, eyeing the pup. "You're too young to have this kind of attitude."

Houdini growled while wagging his tail.

Granny reached in her pocket and pulled something out, giving it to the puppy, who eagerly accepted it.

"What's that?"

"Oh, just something I picked up on the other side."

"Other side?"

"What are you going to do with him?" she asked, changing the subject.

"I suppose I have no choice but to keep him. I can't very well get rid of him." Jerry thought about what Fred had said. "It wouldn't be good if anyone found out about him."

"He's a feisty little fellow. How do you expect to keep him a secret?"

"I don't. Not entirely. I just have to keep the ghost half a secret."

"Do you think that's possible?" Granny asked.

Jerry sighed. "I have no clue. My luck, he will disappear in front of a crowd of people."

Granny reached over and patted him on the arm. "Don't fret – maybe I can have a chat with Gunter and get him to keep the pup in line."

Jerry glanced in the mirror at Gunter. "Is that even possible?"

Granny laughed. "I notice you didn't ask if it was humanly possible. That tells me you know things work differently in my world."

"I wouldn't begin to presume anything about the world you live in. Mostly because you've never shared anything about the other realm." Jerry added.

"That's because it's none of your business. I will, however, have a chat with Gunter to see if we can keep Junior's bloodline under wraps."

"Houdini. It's his name," Jerry offered when

Granny looked at him. "While you're at it, ask for help with housebreaking."

Granny chuckled. "What do you think I am, a miracle worker?"

"There was a time when I would have said yes to that without even stopping to consider the question. I always looked up to you."

"That's because I had you brainwashed into thinking I knew everything there was to know."

"You knew enough."

"If that were the case, you wouldn't have spent most of your life looking for answers."

"Maybe. But then again, isn't that the purpose of life? Searching for the answers to all of life's problems?"

"Sometimes the purpose of life is easing another's burden," Granny said as she placed the puppy in the back.

"What's that supposed to mean?"

"Answer the phone and find out," Granny said as Jerry's cell phone lit up, showing an unknown number. She winked and disappeared as Jerry answered the call.

"McNeal?"

Jerry's heart skipped a beat as he recognized the voice on the other end. "Doc?"

"It's me. How have you been?"

"Doing good, Doc." Jerry passed a small wine shop and resisted the sudden urge to stop. "The question is, how are you?"

"I've had a rough couple of months, but I think I'm making progress. I finally worked up the nerve to call you."

"Worked up the nerve? What's that supposed to mean?"

"I let you down."

"That wasn't you. That was the bottle."

"The bottle doesn't control me. I control me. The bottle didn't hit you. I did, and I called to tell you I'm sorry."

"You don't have to apologize for that."

"I do if I want to beat this thing. It is part of the program, McNeal. I have to take responsibility for my actions. You tried to help me, and I let you down. You were injured. I could have killed you with that punch. You have every right to hang up the phone and never speak to me again."

"We both know that's not going to happen. Let me ask you this, Doc. You've done a lot of soul-searching, right?"

"I have."

"Well, have you ever thought that maybe I was supposed to be there to take that blow?"

"How do you mean?"

"If anyone else would have happened by, you might not have punched them. If you had, you might not have felt as bad. Maybe I was the one put there to make sure you would hit bottom and seek help."

"Dang, McNeal, you're pretty full of yourself, aren't you?"

Jerry smiled. "Just giving you something to think about."

"So you're saying if it weren't for you, I would have died on that mountain."

"I've thought about it. Makes as much sense as anything."

"Well, dang, McNeal, I was going to give you a pat on the back, but your hand is already there. I guess I didn't need to call after all."

"I'm glad you did. It's good to hear your voice, Doc. It's been way too long."

"You good, McNeal?"

"Golden. You good, Doc?"

"No, but I'm moving in the right direction. How about you, McNeal? Are you heading in the right direction?"

Jerry saw the sign welcoming him to Miramar Beach just as Doc asked the question. He smiled into the phone. "I'm about to find out."

"I'm not sure what that means, but I'll leave you with this one bit of advice. Something I've only learned recently. You can't go through life trying to make everyone else happy. You need to find out what makes you happy and expand out from there. Find your happy place, Jerry. I can't tell you where that is, but when you find it, you'll know. I've got to go. I'll check back in when I have more words of wisdom."

Jerry held on to the phone long after Doc ended the call. Jerry didn't know if the universe had somehow known he needed to hear Doc's voice, if Granny had something to do with it or if the timing were merely a fluke, but even now, Doc's voice had a calming effect on him as he pulled into Holly's driveway.

# Chapter Four

Jerry stared at the condo, working up the nerve to knock on the door. It wasn't that he was scared – not of Holly anyway. He just wanted to see if there was anything left of the feeling he'd once felt. He only needed a moment with her – his intuition would tell him the rest. There was a time when he'd thought there was something there, but that was before he'd met April. Since then, it felt as if he were in an invisible game of tug of war. He was tired of playing games and walking on eggshells with April when all he wanted to do was tell her how he felt.

Then there was a part of him that remembered how Holly had looked at him and how he had ached to hold her in his arms and take away her pain. Had that been because he genuinely cared for her, or was it simply because he'd felt guilty over not having found her sooner? Perhaps a bit of both, but what if his feelings for her were real? At the moment, that question prevented him from professing his love to April. He had to know, not only for himself but for April as well. The only chance he had at breaking through her barriers was to make sure there was no voice in the recesses of his mind wondering what if. Max would see it if there were any lingering doubt, and while she cared for him, it wouldn't be enough for her to give her mother the go-ahead to be with him. Even if he tried to block Max from seeing his indecision, she would know and put a stop to it, just like she had in Virginia. And April would listen because she hadn't heeded Max's warning the last time. The only way of getting Max in his corner was to be certain that when he professed his love for April, both would know he was telling the truth.

Jerry looked in the mirror and met Gunter's stare. The dog leaned forward as if asking if he felt it. Jerry did, though he didn't acknowledge it. Just because the visit felt wrong didn't mean he should go. He'd come too far to leave without seeing Holly.

Jerry exited the car and rolled his neck to ease the tension that had his shoulders nearly drawn to his ears. As he reached the door, he looked for Gunter, only to find he had not followed. Jerry wondered if it was because the dog didn't approve of him being there or because he'd chosen to stay back and keep an eye on the pup.

As Jerry placed his finger on the doorbell, he knew the inner turmoil to have been for nothing, as no one was home to open the door. As he removed his finger, the tension left. Jerry returned to his rental car and tapped his fingers on the steering wheel. Anyone else might have left the area never knowing, but Jerry was not like others. Jerry had a way of finding out where Holly had gone. All he had to do was think about her, and his gift would guide him to her as if following a vibration only he could feel.

Jerry turned the small car around in the double driveway and concentrated on finding Holly. Gunter yawned his disapproval. Jerry looked in the mirror. "Knock it off, dog. This doesn't have anything to do with what you want, what Fred thinks, or anything in the other realm. This is my quest, and I'm going to see it through."

Gunter lowered to the backseat emitting a groan as Jerry let off the brake and followed the pull, which led him to the same winery he had passed earlier. Had Jerry not been distracted by Doc's call, he would have recognized the pull for what it was – his inner radar letting him know Holly was inside the building.

Jerry parked in the only space available and headed to the front entrance. Once again, Gunter remained in the vehicle with the puppy. As he reached the steps leading to the entrance, he saw two men sitting on cushioned chairs under the covered porch. One of the men nodded a greeting when Jerry looked in his direction. Jerry returned the nod, and as he reached for the door handle, he received a flash from the night of the blizzard. It showed an elderly man carrying a child. The image cleared, and he looked closer at the older gentleman. Holly's dad. Though Jerry had only seen him briefly when he came into the Chambersburg ER carrying Gracie, he knew it to be him. For a moment, he wondered if perhaps his radar had pinged on Holly's father but knew that was not the case – his inner pull was never wrong. A sadness washed over Jerry as he went inside without further comment.

The interior of the building was much larger than he expected, mainly because the main room was open with a vaulted ceiling that drew the eyes upward. A string of white lights decorated the staircase along the outer wall. The floors were terracotta-colored ceramic tiles that complemented the lighter walls and added to the calm energy within the room. Everywhere he looked was decorated with wine and wine accessories, with a large Christmas tree taking up the center of the room. A woman with shoulder-length brown hair and glasses resting on top of her head smiled at him from behind a long countertop bar. "Welcome to Emerald Coast Wine Cellars. Can I help you find something?"

Jerry shook his head. "No, thank you. Just stopped in to have a look around."

"If you find something you want to try, we have our sampling counter in the back of the room."

Jerry smiled. He doubted the woman would have offered a sample if she had known why he was there. He walked around the room pretending to peruse the tastefully decorated displays of candles, wine, and collectibles as he searched for Holly. While he saw several people milling about the store, he didn't see her, yet his spidey senses told him she was there. *Could it be the spidey senses had been wrong after all?* He walked to the front of the building and peeked out at the two men sitting on the porch. He focused on Holly's dad, then shook his head – the pull didn't come from him. It came from Holly. He heard voices in the other room and walked toward a brightly painted wall that separated the wine area from a small boutique. As soon as he entered, the floor changed from tile to a painted wooden plank, lending to the fun vibe of the room, which was filled with shoes, bold handbags, and colorful clothing that spoke to the Florida lifestyle.

A saleswoman holding several hangers of clothes smiled at him and then spoke to the person on the other side of the dressing room door. "I'll take these to the counter while you get dressed. Is there anything I can help you find, sir?" she asked as she approached Jerry.

He shook his head, and the woman continued on her way. Jerry walked through the room, pretending to look at the items on display and feeling a bit like a creeper when he realized it was all women's clothing. He made his way to the opening that separated the boutique from the wine room, stopping at an old dresser to check out the costume jewelry on display. He saw a pair of ladybug earrings and immediately thought of April. His fingers grazed the enameled insect as he felt more than heard the dressing room door click open.

The hairs on the back of his neck prickled as he turned. His radar told him it was Holly even before she came into view. He'd yearned for this moment for so long, imagining what he would say and how he would react, and yet he said nothing.

Holly looked up and saw him staring at her, her brow creasing. A second later, it lifted as recognition set in. How she recognized him without his shaved head and uniform, he did not know. She had a slight limp, which worsened as she hurried to where he stood, her eyes shining as bright as her smile. She was just as lovely as he remembered, and yet something was missing. Even as she lifted her arms to embrace him, Jerry knew. Or maybe it was his heart, which failed to give that little flutter it produced each time he thought of April.

"Jerry McNeal, what on earth are you doing here?" Holly asked, releasing him.

"I was in the area on business," he fibbed. "I saw this place and thought I'd stop and look around. I have a friend who likes wine," he said by way of explanation.

"Did you get my e-mail? We live close by. You weren't going to leave the area without saying hello, were you?"

"No, I stopped by your condo first, but no one was home."

Her smile grew bolder. "Then it's fate. Why else would you just happen to come into the same shop I'm in?"

*Because my spidey senses led me to you.* Jerry smiled. "Because my friend likes wine?"

The front door opened, and the man who was sitting next to Holly's father came inside. He saw Jerry and Holly talking and went to the tasting bar, and sat at the counter.

Holly finger-waved in the man's direction. The man smiled and returned her wave but made no move to join them. Holly sighed. "I think I owe you an apology. I know I promised to have coffee with you, but the accident freaked me out. I did what I do best and bolted."

Jerry started to tell her it was something they had in common, but she continued her apology.

"I'd planned on calling you, but I got so busy with the move and getting Gracie settled. I did e-mail you a while back, but I never heard from you – I guess you got it because you wouldn't have known where I live if you didn't. I hope you didn't come here expecting something, because I'm involved with someone. I guess it's a good thing we never met up for coffee because it would never have worked out between us."

Jerry wasn't sure how to respond, so he said nothing.

"Anyway, once I got back here, everything kind of turned around for Gracie and me. Gracie's biological father came back into the picture – that's him over there. Things were unsettled between us before, but he's changed. I've changed too. I guess I needed to grow up and quit putting such high expectations on everything."

"There's nothing wrong with expecting someone to treat you with respect," Jerry said, looking at the man.

She shook her head. "It wasn't that he didn't treat me with respect. It was that I overreacted whenever things didn't go perfectly. I found out I was pregnant with Gracie and started giving him ultimatums. Lots of hurtful things were said, and I ran away and refused to allow him any contact with her. My parents divorced when I was a kid, and apparently, I carried that with me into every relationship. While some girls were looking for the glass slipper, I was waiting for the other shoe to drop. Anyway, when I moved back, we hooked up, and when things started to get serious, Ryan insisted we go to couples counseling. I thought he was crazy, but I figured I owed it to Gracie to at least try. I'm glad I did, as it really helped. We are getting married in the spring. Gracie is tickled. Heck, even my dad liked him, and he never liked anyone I dated." A frown tugged at her face. "Dad died a little over a month ago. Heart attack," she said by way of explanation. "I'm so glad he got to meet Ryan, and that Gracie and I were settled here before it happened. Oh, listen to me going on and telling you my life story. How about you? Your sergeant told me you aren't a state trooper anymore. That was a shock. Have you found that thing that makes you happy?"

Jerry thought of April and smiled. "I believe I have."

"I'm sorry. I didn't mean to intrude. It's just that I've always been so cynical when it came to marriage and relationships, and now, I guess I want everyone to find what I've found."

"You didn't intrude. I've been running for a while myself, but now, I think it's time to stop."

"I'm glad, Jerry. You deserve to be happy. Come, I want to introduce you to Ryan." She looped her arm through his before he had a chance to object, leading him to where Ryan sat.

Ryan stood as they approached. If the man had any objections to Holly's affectionate embrace, it didn't show.

Holly kept hold of Jerry's arm. "Ryan, this is Trooper McNeal, the man I told you about. You know, the one with the dog."

Ryan reached for his hand and shook it with great enthusiasm. "I've heard a lot about you, Mr. McNeal. I owe you a great deal for saving my Holly's life."

Jerry pulled his hand from Ryan's grip. "Just doing my job. The main thanks go to the dog. If it wasn't for him, I would have never found her."

At the mention of the dog, Holly's eyes sparkled. "Did you ever find him?"

Before Jerry could answer, Ryan cut in.

"All the same, at least allow me to buy you a drink," he said, looking at the lady behind the tasting counter.

Jerry shook his head. "I'm not much of a wine drinker."

Ryan lifted a brow. "And yet here you are in a wine shop."

"I'm shopping for a friend."

"A lady friend?" Ryan asked.

There was the green-eyed monster Jerry was waiting for. Jerry smiled a disarming smile. "Yes, April is a lovely lady I know in Michigan. I thought maybe I could find her something beachy to break the chill."

Holly turned to the dark-haired woman behind the counter. "You've got to let him try the Sugar Sands White. It is absolutely amazing."

Jerry held up a hand when the woman moved to

grab a glass. "I don't need to sample it. I'll take two bottles. I would like to get a few more while I'm at it. I'm not sure what she likes. But I know she likes wine."

"I'll help," Holly said and sprinted about the room, plucking bottles from the shelves, her limp growing more noticeable as she did. When she returned, she turned the labels where he could see them, reading off their names as she did. "Noble, Sangria Breeze, Beach Berry Breeze. These are some of my favorites. I hope you don't mind."

Jerry shook his head. "Not at all."

"Oh, I forgot one," she said, limping away.

"You weren't just passing through town, were you?" Ryan asked, keeping his voice low.

Jerry saw no reason to lie. "No."

"Then why are you here?"

"Looking for answers."

"Did you find them?"

"I did."

Ryan looked him in the eye. "Do I need to be worried?"

Jerry returned his stare. "Only if you do anything to hurt her or the kid."

Ryan let out a sigh. "Mr. McNeal, I've made a lot of mistakes in my life. Walking away from Holly and not fighting to have Gracie in my life sooner are two of my biggest regrets. I give thanks for them each day and would never do anything to hurt either of them."

Jerry smiled and placed a hand on the man's shoulder, feeling the truth of his words. "Then you'll not have any trouble out of me."

Holly's face was flushed when she returned with a bottle of wine labeled Sherry. "Is this enough, or do you want more?"

Jerry chuckled and nodded to the woman behind the counter, who had gathered the bottles and was awaiting his answer. "I think this is plenty."

Holly hugged Jerry. "Ryan and I were going to grab something to eat. Do you want to join us?"

Jerry shook his head. "No, I'm finished with my business here. I think it's time I head to Michigan."

Ryan's eyes grew wide. "You're not planning on driving to Michigan in that car out front, are you?"

Jerry didn't particularly like the car, but he didn't like this guy harping on his choice of vehicle. He pulled himself taller. "You got a problem with my car?"

Ryan lifted his hands. "Easy, buddy. I don't have an issue with the car. I just don't know how it will hold up with the blizzard making its way across the country."

"Blizzard?" Fred had mentioned a snowstorm but hadn't told him it was a blizzard.

Holly's face paled. "You're not planning on driving in it, are you?"

Jerry shook his head. "No. I'm going to drop off

the rental car and catch a plane as soon as I leave here."

Holly managed a smile. "Oh, good. I still can't look at snow without having an anxiety attack. I think I have PTSD or something because just hearing about the blizzard gets my leg to aching. I haven't limped in weeks, and now I saw the weather report and… I thought it was just because I saw you, and it reminded me of what I went through, but now I'm not so sure. I've seen the weather reports. It's going to be bad."

As the words came out of her mouth, Jerry felt a chill race the length of his spine.

# Chapter Five

Jerry hurried to the front door of the winery feeling as if a weight had been lifted from his shoulders. Any feelings he'd had for Holly were in the past, and it helped to know she was in a good place. He was also happy she'd found someone to spend her life with. Now, if he could only get his own life in order.

Jerry opened the door and looked to where Holly's dad sat, thinking to bid him a good day. He stopped short at seeing Holly's dad, Calvin Wood, running a ghostly hand the length of the shepherd pup.

Gunter stood watching over them and looked up when Jerry stepped beside him.

Calvin looked up at Jerry and smiled. "These two

belong to you?"

Jerry nodded. "They do."

"I thought so." He nodded to Gunter. "I figure that one can take care of himself, but I was worried about this little guy. I saw the crate in the backseat and tried to put him back inside, but he got out again. I thought he might have fallen out the window, but it wasn't open enough for that to happen."

Jerry smiled. "He's a bit of an escape artist. That's why I call him Houdini."

"It fits. Funny how he didn't follow you inside."

"I must have been too fast for him." Jerry didn't like skipping around the truth, but he didn't think it prudent to let the spirit world know that Gunter was the father. That Granny hadn't known meant the rest probably didn't either, and he thought to keep it that way.

"You should keep a closer watch on him. If he had gone to the road, he would have been a goner."

Jerry looked at Gunter, knowing the ghostly K-9 wouldn't have let that happen. "Thank you for looking out for him."

"You'd better take him away before my daughter comes out and sees him. She's had her heart set on a German shepherd ever since one saved her life. She's been scouring the internet looking for one with the exact markings of the one that helped her. This little guy seems to fit the bill." Calvin looked the pup over and held him up to Jerry.

*That's because he shares his DNA.* Jerry hurried to block the spirit from reading his thoughts as he took Houdini from him. Houdini wriggled in his arms and angled to slather him with puppy kisses as Jerry tried unsuccessfully to keep his face out of reach. "Yes, sir, his father was quite the stud."

Gunter smiled a K-9 smile.

"You wouldn't be inclined to sell him to her, would you?"

Gunter's smile evaporated.

Jerry shook his head. "No, sir. I'm afraid I'm already pretty attached to this guy."

"Are there any more in the litter?"

*Good question* – one Jerry still didn't have an answer to. "No, sir. This one is the only one."

"You'd better not say anything to my daughter, then."

"I'll do my part and get him out of sight before she comes out," Jerry said, turning.

The spirit's energy flickered. "I didn't say she was inside."

"No, you didn't." Jerry smiled and offered his hand. "Jerry McNeal."

The spirit's energy brightened. "The same Trooper McNeal who saved my daughter's life?"

"Used to be. It's just Jerry now. Nice to see you again, Mr. Wood."

Calvin's brow creased. "Again?"

"We haven't been introduced. I was in the ER

when you came in. You were carrying Gracie," Jerry told him. In reality, the only reason Jerry knew the man's first name was because he'd done some extra investigating on his own.

Calvin looked at Gunter. "Holly said it was your dog that saved her. This looks like the dog in the photo, so I assume it's the same dog. Was he alive then?"

*Tread carefully, McNeal.* "No, sir. That is why I was surprised when Holly was able to see him. Can she see you?"

Calvin shook his head. "No, she talks to me. But I can tell she is just speaking to my memory. You said he was dead?"

"Yes, sir."

"And yet she was able to capture a photo of him. I knew she was a good photographer, but how is that possible?"

Jerry shrugged. "I've asked myself that numerous times."

Calvin eyed the puppy. "Strange how much he looks like that big dog."

"That's what drew me to him. As soon as I laid eyes on the pup, he reminded me of the dog, and I knew I was destined to have him. I guess I'd better be on my way before Holly sees him and decides to fight me for him."

Calvin smiled. "My money would be on Holly, gimpy leg and all."

"Mine too, sir. Your daughter is a fighter. No doubt about that. Not many could have survived that wreck."

"She wouldn't have either if not for that dog. She calls him her angel. I guess she's right about that."

Jerry gave a quick glance to Gunter, who had regained his smile. "Yes, sir. The dog is a real hero."

Gunter wagged his tail.

"Is there anything I can do for you, Mr. Wood?"

"For me?"

"I can talk to Holly if you want. Give her a message?"

Calvin was quiet for a moment, then shook his head. "No, it wouldn't do any good for her to know I'm here. She'd keep talking, and I'd have no way to answer her. I'm okay with the way things are. That fellow she's with is good to both her and Gracie. That's good enough for me."

*For me too.* "I'm happy to know she has an angel of her own to watch over her, but just so you know, you don't have to stay here."

"I've looked after her my whole life – I don't intend on stopping just because I'm dead." He looked toward the entrance. "She'll be out soon. You'd best be on your way."

"Roger that, sir." Jerry hurried down the steps and put Houdini back inside the crate. "Stay."

Houdini tried to push through the bars. Jerry placed out a hand to stop him and looked over at

Gunter as he appeared beside him. "I thought you were supposed to be watching him."

Gunter yawned and looked at him as if to say, *I'm doing my best.*

Jerry laughed. "Mike said a tired dog is a good dog. What do you say we wear the little fellow out a bit?"

Gunter barked his approval. Jerry laughed when the pup gave a woof of his own.

"Okay then, the beach it is!" Jerry drove up Scenic Highway and found a parking spot just past the Whale's Tail Restaurant. He retrieved the puppy from the crate and pulled a few doggie waste bags from the roll, and shoved them in his pocket. Gunter stayed by his side until they reached the sand. He spotted the water, ran ahead, and darted into the waves. The pup squirmed to go after him, but Jerry carried him until they were closer to the water. The second his feet hit the sand, Houdini bolted toward Gunter, stopping when the first wave grew close. He sank down just out of its reach and barked. The wave retreated, and Houdini stood looking rather proud of himself for having chased it away. He started forward, the wave returned, and the pup raced back to the safety of the dry sand. Jerry laughed as Houdini squared his shoulders, once again challenging the water's advance.

The pup continued the game for several moments until he turned and took off running in the opposite direction. Jerry gave chase, stopping when he saw what had captured the puppy's attention. A large crab crawled sideways in the sand, pinchers raised, daring the pup to come closer. Houdini lurched forward, darting to the side as the crab snapped his claws. Unfazed, Houdini stalked the crab, lowering to the sand and emitting puppy growls. The crab waltzed to the side, claws at the ready. Each time the pup would near the crab, he planted himself and prepared for a fight.

Jerry snapped a few photos of the standoff, smiling when the puppy was visible on the screen. The crab inched to the side and disappeared into a hole in the sand. Houdini raced forward, sniffed the opening, then began digging for all he was worth. Gunter raced from the water and joined the effort.

Jerry switched to video. *Max is going to love this.* As he filmed, Jerry recalled the way Max's face lit up whenever she was around Gunter. *The puppy! She would love him.*

Gunter woofed.

Jerry looked to see the dog staring directly at him. He stopped recording. "Is that it? Did you bring me the pup so I could take him to Max?"

Gunter spun in a circle, wagging his tail.

"Is that why you didn't go inside with me when I went to speak to Holly?"

Gunter woofed again. Houdini stopped digging, sank to the sand, and emitted a high-pitched bark.

Jerry chuckled at the pup's antics then looked at Gunter. "You sure are one smart dog. You knew where my heart lay even before I was sure. Wait until I tell Max I got her a puppy."

Gunter stilled his tail and growled a low growl.

"We?"

Gunter lifted his lip into a smile.

Jerry swiped through his phone, stopping when he saw April's number. "I guess I'd better clear it with her mother first. Then again, the three of us are pretty much a package deal." Jerry frowned. *What if April doesn't want us? Sheesh, McNeal, you're acting like a schoolboy. Just call the woman, profess your love and get it over with.* Jerry firmed his chin, deciding to make the call.

"Jerry! I was just thinking of you."

Jerry's heart warmed. "You were?"

"Yes, I need a good detective."

He tightened his grip on the phone. "What's wrong?"

"It's Max."

"Max? What's wrong with Max?"

"Her birthday is coming up. I had her present lined up, and it disappeared."

"Must be some present if you're willing to hire a detective. You know Max is gifted, right? Maybe you should tell her what it is and let her find it for you."

"I thought about it, but I wanted it to be a

surprise. Now I'll have to find something else, and I have no clue what to get her."

Jerry's smile returned as he looked at the puppy. *Perfect timing.* "What were you going to get her?"

"A puppy."

The hairs on the back of Jerry's neck stood on end.

April continued. "I know how much she enjoys having Gunter around. She's old enough to help take care of one, and to be honest, I would like the security of having a dog around."

Jerry swallowed and looked at Houdini. "You said you had one picked out, and it disappeared?"

"Yes, but in reality, someone likely stole it. The puppies were out in the yard with their mother, and the one I had chosen for Max went missing. Jeff said he only left them alone for a couple of minutes. He doesn't know if someone stole the pup or if a hawk carried it off."

"This Jeff you're talking about – Jeff Mills, right?"

"That's right, from the campground. His dog Lady had pups. I forgot you knew him."

"April, what color was the pup?"

She sighed through the phone. "He looked just like Gunter. That's why I chose him. All the other pups are black."

"What if I told you that you were right the first time."

"What do you mean?"

"When you said the pup disappeared."

"I'm not following you, Jerry."

"I've got your puppy." There was no reason to beat around the bush. It was the only explanation.

"What do you mean you have my puppy?"

"He showed up at my parents' house a couple days ago."

"Jerry, your parents live in Florida. The puppy was in Michigan – how did he get to Florida?"

"Gunter brought him."

"I don't understand. How would Gunter even know about the puppies?"

Jerry started to ask if she was sitting down.

"Jerry, please stop making me ask. Tell me what's going on."

"When we were in Michigan, Gunter took a special liking to Lady."

"Are you trying to tell me that Gunter got Lady pregnant?"

"As crazy as it sounds, that is exactly what I'm saying."

"Jerry, Gunter is a ghost."

"I didn't say I understand it. I'm just saying this puppy is…"

"Dead?"

Jerry looked at the puppy, who was now rolling in the sand. "No, Houdini is very much alive."

"Houdini?"

"It seemed fitting."

"But if he's alive, how can you be sure Gunter's the father?"

"Because he has escaped from both his crate and the car while the doors were closed."

"Houdini," April repeated, getting the reference.

Jerry laughed. "The name fits."

"Maybe it's a good thing we're not getting him. God knows how much trouble a puppy like that would be to take care of."

Jerry's heart sank.

"Jerry? Are you still there?"

"I'm here."

"You got quiet."

*Tell her, Jer.* "I was just thinking."

"About?"

"I was trying to gather the nerve to tell you why I called."

April laughed a carefree laugh. "Well, now you have to tell."

"I was calling to ask if I could give Max a puppy, but since you don't want him."

"Of course, I want him."

"You just said."

"I only said that because I didn't want you to feel bad about having him. How will you get him here? It's too cold to ship him."

It was Jerry's turn to laugh. "I wouldn't think of shipping him. He'd probably escape from the crate and fall out of the cargo hold of the plane. I was thinking about bringing him myself."

"You're still in Florida, aren't you?"

"Yes."

"It's a long drive, and we have a blizzard watch."

"Then I guess I'd better hurry and book a flight."

"Oh, Jerry, Max is going to be thrilled. Not only with the puppy, but with seeing you again."

"How about you, April? Will you be glad to see me?"

The line grew quiet.

"April?"

"I'm here," she said softly.

"I'll see you soon, okay?"

Her voice grew strong once more. "Do me a favor."

*Anything.* "What's that?"

"Don't try to be a hero. If the weather gets too bad, turn around."

"Don't you worry about me, April. I'm a veteran driver."

"I'm serious, Jerry."

"So am I. Besides, I'll be flying most of the way. Speaking of which, I'd better see about getting a flight."

"Good luck. A lot of airlines are already canceling flights."

"Oh, ye of little faith. Are you forgetting my ace in the hole?"

April laughed. "Which is?"

"Fred."

Another laugh. "Good ole Uncle Fred."

Jerry peered at the phone. "Uncle Fred?"

"That's what Max calls him."

Jerry chuckled. "How is Max? I haven't heard from her in a bit."

"She's good."

"Why do I get the feeling there's a but in there?"

"No, but. I just told her we needed to give you some space."

"What if I don't want any space?"

"You drive safe, Jerry." The screen flashed, showing the call had ended.

"I won't let you push me away again," Jerry said, slipping the phone into his pocket.

# Chapter Six

Jerry took Houdini to the do-it-yourself dog wash to remove all the sand. While the pup wasn't thrilled with getting a bath, the task was easier than Jerry had expected. He'd just finished blow-drying him and putting him back inside his crate when his cell rang, showing Fred's call.

Jerry swiped to answer the call as he started back to his car. "I was just about to call you."

"I know, April called me."

"April?"

"She's worried about you driving in the blizzard and wanted me to try to talk some sense into you."

Jerry put the crate in the back, and to his relief, the pup seemed content to stay inside. Gunter must have agreed, as he took his place in the front passenger seat instead of the back. "Did you remind her that I've driven in snow before?"

"I told her you are in love with her, and nothing is going to stop you from seeing her."

Jerry's mouth went dry. Sure, he felt it, but he thought he would be the one to actually tell her.

Fred laughed when Jerry failed to reply. "Breathe, McNeal. All I told her was that you used to be a Pennsylvania state trooper and have driven in your fair share of storms."

Jerry found his voice. "Did that ease her mind?"

"Nope. She proceeded to tell me this is a blizzard and not a storm."

"Jeez."

"You should be happy she cares enough to be worried. Speaking of caring, if you're going to see them, does that mean things didn't go well with your friend in Florida?"

"Things went just as I'd hoped they would."

"Good, because if you ask me, you and the Buchanans belong together."

"I didn't ask you."

"No, but if you did, that is what I'd tell you."

"April said Max calls you Uncle Fred. Personally, I think you sound more like Dear Abby. You're my boss, Fred. Not my counselor." The truth of the matter was that Fred wasn't telling him anything he didn't already know. But just because he felt it didn't mean he wasn't worried that April would reject him again. She had hung up on him after all.

"Just trying to help."

"If you want to help, I'd like to have my ride back."

"I've been working on that. I can get you a flight to Nashville on a commercial flight today and have your Durango waiting for you, or I might be able to get you both to Detroit tomorrow."

"Might be able?"

"Depends on the storm. The boys flying the plane don't want to get stranded in the Motor City."

"What do they have against Detroit?"

Fred laughed. "Their wives aren't there."

"Understood. Get me into Nashville, and I'll take it from there."

"I'm going to have to get special permission for that arsenal you travel with."

"Don't worry about that. I left the bag with my pop. I just have my 9mm."

"Okay, that will make it easier. Oh, and, McNeal, at the risk of butting in, April's right. This storm is formidable."

"Or it could just be hype. It happens all the time."

"Not this time, McNeal. Our weather guys are all over it. They say it's going to be bad."

Jerry rubbed the back of his neck. "I know you think this is just about my getting to April, and a big part of it is, but I think there's more to it. My radar started pinging the minute I heard about the storm. I don't know the why of it, but I know I need to head in that direction."

"It's your call, McNeal. You know this stuff better than anyone. That's why I wanted you on our team. You head over to the airport, and I'll get you a seat on the next plane out."

Jerry looked at Gunter. "Any chance of making that two seats? The dogs don't like to share."

"Consider it done."

"Thanks."

Fred laughed. "So the puppy's still with you?"

"He is." Jerry started to tell him what April said about there being more in the litter but decided to keep that information to himself for the time being. While he liked Fred, the man was the head of an agency that sometimes used questionable tactics to get what they wanted, and something told him Fred would insist on getting his hands on all the pups.

"Okay, head over to Pensacola Airport, and I'll get you on a flight to Nashville. It's the best I can do today. I'll text you your itinerary as soon as I get it," Fred said and ended the call.

Jerry looked at Gunter. "I guess we're going to fly."

Gunter smiled, causing the hairs on the back of his neck to stand on end. Jerry narrowed his eyes. "Air travel is serious business. I need you to promise me you will be on your best behavior."

Gunter cocked his head to the side as his smile grew wider.

\*\*\*

Jerry's badge made getting through security with a handgun a nonissue. Even Houdini cooperated, content to remain in his carrier and let Jerry enjoy a rare moment of normalcy, if, in fact, one considered "normal" walking through airport security with one and a half ghostly companions traveling with him. He made his way to his gate, getting the occasional stare from the rare individual whose second glance let him know they'd seen Gunter. The reactions varied. A subtle nod or smile went a long way to letting him know he'd just encountered a kindred spirit. A raised eyebrow led him to think the person was shocked to see such a well-behaved K-9 walking unrestrained in a public setting. A woman in a canary yellow top that elicited an image of Big Bird hurried toward him with a deep scowl. Jerry sighed. And then there was the frown. Oh, how he hated the frown. He lengthened his stride, doing his best to avoid eye contact as the woman approached.

"What gives you the right to walk through this airport with an untethered dog?" she asked as she caught up to him.

Jerry thought about showing her his badge, but having seen her type before, knew better than to engage her. The woman didn't work for the airport, so it wouldn't matter. Ignoring her, he continued without comment.

"Don't walk away when I'm talking to you," she said, grabbing hold of his arm.

Gunter growled, and she released his arm.

"See, that's what I'm talking about. It's obvious he is not a service dog because they are trained not to growl. He's a vicious beast and shouldn't be in the airport, much less without a leash. Why doesn't he have a muzzle? If he was my dog, he'd be wearing a muzzle."

"If he was your dog, he'd run away," Jerry countered.

"How dare you!" she fumed.

"Ma'am, I don't want any trouble. I am just trying to catch my flight. Do you have a flight to catch? I'd hate for you to miss it on account of me."

"Was that a threat? It sounded like a threat."

"Ma'am, I'm not threatening you. I just don't want you to miss your flight."

The woman's frown deepened. "Don't tell me what I should or shouldn't be doing. Where I'm going is my business, and I'll thank you to stay out of it."

"Enough!" Jerry stopped walking, and the woman nearly fell into him. He used his cop voice, keeping his words nice and even. "You are the one who is butting your nose in where it doesn't belong. Turn yourself around and be off to wherever it was you were going before you decided to get up in my business."

"Well, I never."

"I doubt that."

She narrowed her eyes at him. "You are rude!"

"And you, lady, are a…" Jerry took a calming breath. "Have a good day, ma'am."

"I'm going to call security on you," she called after him when he walked away.

*Don't do it, McNeal.* Jerry turned and told her his gate number then rounded and continued on his way. Once out of earshot, Jerry looked at Gunter. "I think I handled that rather well."

Gunter growled a deep growl.

"I know I gave her my gate number. I hope they do look at the security tapes. It's not like they will see you." Jerry smiled. "You're probably right. Next time, I'll just let you bite her."

Gunter's growl turned into a K-9 smile.

"There's our gate. Looks like we still have a few minutes before we start boarding." Jerry found an empty seat and placed the dog carrier at his feet. Gunter stood next to him, fixated on two little girls who were playing near the window. Wearing matching pink outfits, their hair wove about their head in intricate braids capped off with beads that matched their clothing. Jerry turned the crate to allow the puppy to watch as he called Fred.

"McNeal? Is there a problem with your

itinerary?"

"Nope, everything looks good. I just wanted to say thank you for giving them the heads-up I'd be coming."

"Not sure what you mean."

"I thought maybe you'd made one of your special phone calls, as I didn't have any trouble passing through security with my service weapon."

"Did you show them your badge?"

"I did."

"Then why would you expect trouble?"

"Because a part of me thought the badge was all smoke and mirrors. Seriously, Lead Paranormal Investigator?"

"McNeal, I'm beginning to think the military wasted a lot of money on shrinks with you."

Jerry laughed. "Tell me about it. So, you're telling me this is all legit."

"Your bank account should have already told you that," Fred said dryly.

Jerry shrugged. "I don't check my account very often."

A sigh floated through the phone. "Not for nothing, McNeal, but I sure hope this thing with April and Max works out."

"Why's that?"

"Because you need a good woman to help ground you."

Jerry laughed. "Says the man who just bought

me a ticket to get on a plane."

"What can I say? I'm a romantic at heart."

Jerry heard giggles and looked to see that Houdini had made his way out of the crate and was trying his best to catch hold of one of the younger girl's braids. The older of the two girls held out a stuffed bear, and the pup jumped. She pulled it away just before he caught hold, and Houdini sank into a playful bow, woofing and wiggling his delight at having found playmates close to his size.

Jerry looked up and saw airport security heading in his direction. "I've got to go."

"Problem?"

"I think I can handle it, but you should probably keep your phone close just in case I'm wrong." Jerry switched off his cell, stepped across the aisle, and scooped up the pup. Houdini whined and tried to squirm free as the girls begged Jerry to allow him to stay. Jerry nodded to the man who'd just approached. "Sorry, girls, airport security says no."

"But he's so cute," the younger of the two replied.

The child's mother shushed her. "Leave that man alone, Shantel. He told you no."

Jerry smiled at the guard as he put the puppy inside the crate and blocked his way from escaping. "I guess you wouldn't believe me if I told you he escaped."

The guard's face remained stoic. "Not likely

since we received a call saying you were allowing him to walk free while walking to your terminal. Granted, from the woman's call, I expected him to be bigger."

Jerry shrugged. "I'm not sure who called, but I can guarantee this puppy was in his crate until just a couple of moments ago. You don't believe me, check the cameras."

"That won't be necessary. Just keep him locked up unless you are in the designated area."

"I'll keep a better eye on him," Jerry promised as they called for the first to board. He held up his ticket. "I'd better get in line."

The security guard nodded and stepped aside.

Jerry scooped up the crate along with his carry-on and stepped into line. He looked down at Gunter. "Way to go, dude. You're supposed to be keeping an eye on him."

Gunter yawned.

"Don't give me any of that deadbeat father crap. He's your kid, and that makes him your responsibility."

The woman behind him cleared her throat.

Jerry turned, and she raised an eyebrow. He shrugged and smiled a sheepish smile. "Sorry, just practicing what I'm going to say to my nephew when I see him."

The woman crossed her arms, bringing her cleavage together.

Jerry averted his eyes. The woman huffed and looked down her nose at him as she turned her attention to her phone.

Jerry resisted a smile as Gunter moved next to the woman, placing his paw on the toe of her shoe. Her eyes grew wide as she tried to move her foot. Jerry tapped the side of his leg to call the dog off and smiled as he turned away from her. He heard a man's voice and looked behind him to see a man standing where the woman had been only a few seconds earlier. He glanced around the man to see the woman heading to the back of the line. Jerry ran a hand over his head. *Keep it up, McNeal, and you'll get kicked off the flight before you even leave the terminal.*

# Chapter Seven

The couple in front of him cleared the check-in, and Jerry handed the attendant his tickets. He held up the crate when the attendant paused at the second ticket. She took part of the voucher and handed him the rest.

Jerry hurried through the connecting tunnel, half expecting to be called back. The woman traveling with the two little girls sat in the row in front of him. Both girls giggled as he walked past. Jerry's tickets were for the middle and window seats. Jerry motioned Gunter to the window seat, placed his bag overhead, and sat beside the dog, acting as a barrier to whoever sat in the aisle seat. He kept the carrier in his lap as the passengers continued to board, watching and wondering who would take the seat next to him.

He glimpsed something yellow and laughed at the irony. *That would be my luck to have the woman from my encounter in the terminal sitting next to me.* The yellow shirt moved closer and proved not to be the woman in question. Jerry sighed his relief. The woman who'd been standing behind him in line at the gate entered the plane and slowed when she neared.

Jerry watched her from the corner of his eye. *Please don't let it be her.*

The woman checked her ticket against the numbers overhead, blew out a relieved sigh, and hoisted her bag into the overhead compartment on the opposite side. She sat in the seat closest to the aisle and immediately started typing away on her phone.

The aisle traffic cleared. Jerry heard a faint click and looked over in time to see the woman snapping a photo of him.

Realizing she'd been caught, she lowered her phone and began typing once more.

Jerry chuckled, leaned close to Gunter, and lowered his voice. "Probably telling the person on the other end she's sitting next to a crazy guy."

Gunter growled.

"It's okay, boy. I'm getting used to it." A flight attendant moved to close the cabin door. Jerry smiled and placed Houdini's crate in the empty seat to his left. Even though Houdini was a pup, he felt comforted by having both German shepherds flanking him. The calming presence was welcomed, as the last time he'd been on a plane was when he'd flown to Tennessee for his grandmother's funeral. Jerry draped his hand over the carrier to prevent the pup from escaping and closed his eyes.

Gunter snorted.

Jerry opened his eyes to see an attendant standing in the aisle with a beverage cart and realized he'd fallen asleep.

The attendant offered a smile. "Would you like something?"

"Ginger ale."

Gunter smacked his lips.

"And cookies if you have them."

The attendant nodded and handed Jerry a cup of ice and his drink then handed over two packages of wafers. "In case you plan on sharing with the pup."

Jerry thanked the man and waited for him to move on before opening the package and sharing with both Gunter and Houdini. He felt someone watching him and looked to see it was the woman in the seat across the aisle.

Granny's voice drifted through his thoughts. *Give her the bird.*

*I'll do no such thing,* Jerry said, using his inner thoughts to communicate with his grandmother's spirit.

*At least stick your tongue out at her.*

Jerry had to give it to the woman – she hadn't lost any of her spunk since leaving the world. *You know, the last time I flew was when I went to your funeral.*

*I thought that might bother you, so I decided to drop in for a visit.*

*Where are you?*

*Just in your mind. I can appear if you'd like.*

"No!" Jerry heard an intake of air and realized he'd voiced the comment out loud. He looked over at the woman and smiled.

Her face remained stoic as she reached up and pushed the call button. A moment later, a flight attendant stopped at her seat and leaned in close while the woman whispered something in her ear. The attendant straightened, walked away, and then casually returned. This time she turned her attention to Jerry. "Are you alright, sir?"

That she thought walking away and coming back would throw him off the trail of who'd complained made him laugh. "Never better."

The attendant smiled. "Are you sure?"

Jerry crooked a finger and motioned her closer.

The woman leaned forward, and Jerry lowered his voice to a whisper. "Did she tell you I was talking to myself?"

The attendant nodded.

Jerry took note of her nametag – Roni. "I figured

as much. Here's the deal, Roni. The woman is my ex. She found out I'd booked this trip and booked herself on the same flight out of spite."

Roni blinked her surprise. "Oh, my. Maybe I should ask her if she wants to change seats. There is an empty seat in the back of the plane."

Jerry shook his head. "No, she'd most likely deny knowing me. The last time this happened, she made a big scene. There's no reason to disturb the other passengers. I just wanted to let you know in case she says anything else."

"I understand, sir." Roni started to leave and hesitated. "Would you like to move?"

Jerry used his hands to point out the empty seats. "No, I like my space. Besides, it's the principle of the thing. If I give up my seat, she's won."

Roni smiled her understanding. "If you change your mind, just let me know."

"I will."

The moment the attendant walked away, Granny continued their conversation. *Oh, Jerry, that was so much fun. I wish you would have let the woman try to move her.*

*Nah, she would have told the attendant the truth, and there would have been a big uproar. The airlines frown on that kind of thing. It wouldn't look too good if I ended up being the reason the whole plane got detoured.*

*The plane is almost to Atlanta. They wouldn't*

*detour it now.*

*True. But they could detain me, and I only have thirty minutes to catch my connecting flight once we land.*

*I'm glad you picked April, Jerry. I like her and Max.*

*I do too, Granny. I wish you could have met them.*

*I've met Max.*

*I know, she told me. I just wish you could have met her when you were still alive.*

*Don't you worry about Max. Once your parents meet her, they will fall in love with both her and April. I'm glad you had a nice visit with your parents.*

Jerry smiled. *So am I.*

*They're not getting any younger. Don't wait so long to see them.*

*Do you know something you're not telling me?* Jerry searched her mind, looking for answers she didn't share.

*No, Jerry. I just don't want you to have any regrets when the time finally comes.*

The energy around him changed, and he knew his grandmother had left.

The in-plane intercom crackled to life. "Ladies and gentlemen, this is your captain speaking. We will be arriving in Atlanta in about twelve minutes. The current time is four fifty-two p.m., and it is a balmy sixty-eight degrees. A lot of the Midwest flights have been canceled due to a blizzard heading in from the west. Safe travels to everyone who finds themselves in the storm's path."

The moment the captain mentioned the storm, the hairs on the back of Jerry's neck stood on end. He had a flash of a woman crying out in pain. The vision cleared and was replaced by a large grey wall. Behind the wall was a mountain of snow. The vision cleared just as quickly as it appeared. Jerry blew out a long breath. Gunter placed his muzzle on Jerry's shoulder. Jerry reached up, placing a hand on the dog's head. "I'm glad you're here," Jerry whispered and ducked out of the way as Gunter snaked his tongue into his ear. He turned his head and saw the woman across from him glaring at him. Jerry resisted the urge to stick out his tongue.

\*\*\*

While Jerry's upbringing demanded he allow the woman to exit first, he made no offer to help retrieve her bag. Instead, he stood waiting inside his space while the woman grabbed her bag, then bid her silent good riddance as she hurried from the plane.

Jerry stepped into the aisle, fished his bag out of the overhead compartment, then picked up the puppy crate. He stepped back long enough to allow Gunter into the walkway and followed the dog from the plane. His phone chimed. Jerry looked to see a message from Fred. > *How was your flight?*

Jerry hit reply and typed as he walked. > *Remind me to drive next time.*

Fred. > *Turbulence?*

Jerry stepped around a woman, typed another message and hit send. > *People.*

Fred. > *Next time, give me a little more warning, and I'll see you have a private plane. Hang in there, and whatever you do, don't miss your next flight. Everything else is canceled or in the process of being canceled. You miss this one, and you'll spend at least three nights in Atlanta.*

Jerry sent a reply letting Fred know he understood and pocketed his phone. "Yo, dog, let's roll!" Jerry started into a jog, weaving in and out of the crowd. Gunter skirted around him, and suddenly, a path opened, allowing Jerry to move in a straight line. They reached his gate as the PA was announcing last call for boarding.

Jerry handed the woman his tickets, and the woman frowned. Jerry glanced at the ticket. "Problem?"

"No, it's just there are several people on standby that could use that extra seat of yours."

Jerry shook his head. "Not going to happen. That seat is for my service dog." *Okay, it's sort of the truth.*

The woman looked at the small carrier and raised an eyebrow.

"He's a puppy."

"Puppies can't be service dogs. They're not old enough," she countered.

Jerry shrugged. "He's in training."

The woman firmed her chin. Jerry was just getting ready to pull out his badge when the other attendant spoke up.

"Let him on. There's no time to change anything anyway."

Jerry headed to the door, and the woman called out to him. Jerry turned, badge in hand, ready to end the discussion.

The woman held up his ticket. "You might need this."

Jerry retrieved his tickets and then hurried through the connecting tunnel. The moment he stepped inside the airplane cabin, the attendant closed the door behind him.

"You're a lucky one."

Jerry smiled. "That's what they tell me." He scanned his ticket to find his seat number and searched the overhead to find the correlating number. As his gaze drifted down, he sucked in his breath. The woman he had claimed was his ex was sitting in the aisle seat in the same row he'd been assigned.

Her lips pinched together as she shook her head. "Oh no. You're not sitting here."

"Afraid so," Jerry replied. He sat the crate on the floor and lifted his carry-on to the overhead compartment then looked at the woman.

She crossed her arms, stretching her legs to keep him from claiming his seat. Gunter stretched, invading the woman's personal space. She pulled her legs back and batted the air. "What was that?"

Jerry hid a smile. "I have no clue what you're talking about."

"Sir, you need to take your seat."

Jerry turned toward the flight attendant. "I'll be glad to if this lady would be so kind as to allow me in."

They both looked at the woman, who shook her head. "I'm not sitting by him. He's weird and talks to himself. He can sit somewhere else."

The attendant moved in front of Jerry. "There are no other seats. This flight is full. To be honest, I'm surprised that one is empty."

Jerry looked at the seat in question, which technically wasn't empty as Gunter was now sitting there smiling a K-9 grin. "That seat also belongs to me. I have the ticket right here."

"He's not sitting here."

"Just let him sit down so we can leave," someone yelled from further back in the plane.

A second flight attendant stepped forward. "Ma'am, either you let him have his seat, or we will escort you from the plane."

The woman's eyes grew wide. "Me? Why should I leave?"

"Because you're the one holding up the plane. Last chance. Let him sit, or we take you off."

The woman let out a disgusted sigh. "Fine, he can sit." She looked at Jerry. "BY THE WINDOW."

Jerry looked at Gunter, who smiled a K-9 smile and moved to the center seat. Jerry stooped to pick up the crate. It was too light. He eased open the grate and lifted it from the ground.

"Sir, you need to have a seat."

Jerry smiled a sheepish grin. "I can't."

"Why not?"

He held up the crate. "It seems my puppy has escaped."

He felt a tug on his arm and looked to see one of the little girls from the previous flight standing beside him holding Houdini.

"Momma said I had to bring him back." She shrugged. "He wanted to sit with me."

The head flight attendant took the puppy from her and handed him to Jerry. Either she was not a fan of dogs or was tired of the delay. Either way, the crease between her brow told him she was not in the mood for any more games. She narrowed her eyes at Jerry. "You are to have a seat, and this puppy is to remain in his crate."

Jerry edged his way past the woman, claimed his seat next to the window, and placed the crate in his lap.

The flight attendant shook her head. "Either

under the seat or in the seat next to you during takeoff."

The carrier was too big to fit under the seat. As he moved to place it in the seat beside him, Gunter disappeared.

Houdini whined.

The woman beside him crossed her arms. "I am not going to listen to that the whole flight."

Jerry started to tell the woman that the pup was merely upset at the hostile energy she was emitting but doubted that would help the situation. Instead, he stuck his fingers inside the crate. Houdini seemed pleased with this new game and instantly began chewing on them.

"Are we good here?" the flight attendant asked, her tone letting them know neither had better say otherwise.

The woman sitting next to him shrugged her indifference.

The flight attendant started to walk away and paused, looking them each in the eye. "The flight is just over an hour. Don't make me regret not kicking you both off the plane when I had the chance."

"If you touch me, I'll have you arrested," the woman whispered the moment the flight attendant left.

Jerry reached into his pocket and pulled out his badge, flashing it in her direction without so much as a sideways glance. Returning the badge to his pocket, he removed his fingers from the crate, draped his arm so that his fingers were blocking the opening, and closed his eyes. As Jerry drifted off to sleep, he felt a tingle on the back of his neck.

# Chapter Eight

After the initial chaos, the remainder of the flight proved uneventful. The woman beside him kept to herself. Even though Gunter hadn't shown himself, Jerry felt the dog was near. That Houdini had remained quiet for the flight led Jerry to believe that he, too, felt Gunter's calming presence. Still, even with the outward calm, Jerry felt something off. He chanced a sideways glance at the woman to his left, surprised when she offered him a sweet smile.

*Maybe she's one of those badge bunnies June wrote about. Doubtful. Still, something had changed. Perhaps if he had shown her the badge earlier, all of the craziness could have been avoided. It couldn't have been that easy.* Jerry drummed his fingers on the arm of his chair. *Something's off.* He knew that to be the case, as the crawling sensation on the back of his neck was never wrong. *Come on, McNeal, what are you missing?*

The captain came on, letting them know they'd started their descent and would be landing shortly. The woman sitting next to him looked at him, smiled, and bit her lower lip.

*Okay, lady, what's got you so giddy? Don't read anything into it, McNeal. She's probably meeting someone and is excited about seeing them. Maybe, but there is more to it.* He couldn't help being cynical; the woman had rubbed him the wrong way from the moment he'd laid eyes on her. *What is it that bothers you so much, McNeal? I don't know. I just don't like her. Could it be because you think she is right? Let's face it, you are weird, not to mention that you are sitting here at this very moment having a conversation with yourself.*

"Sir?"

Jerry looked to see a flight attendant standing in the aisle, staring at him. "Yes?"

"It is my understanding that you are a police officer?"

Jerry glanced at the woman in the row with him. "Something like that."

The lady in the seat glanced at him and then looked away as the flight attendant leaned closer and lowered her voice. "We've had some trouble at the back of the plane. We have the situation under control at present, but we need to take the man into custody."

*Crap. There must be a code on the ticket that shows I'm on the job. Makes sense they'd want to know in case of trouble.* Jerry reached to unbuckle his seatbelt.

The attendant stopped him. "Not yet. We have the man subdued and don't want to alarm the rest of the passengers. We were hoping you would agree to remain in your seat until the rest of the passengers departed and then go back and take custody of the man until authorities arrive."

Something didn't smell right. Maybe it was because the woman sitting next to him hadn't looked in his direction once since the attendant began speaking. He could understand her looking at the attendant while she spoke, but why hadn't she turned toward him to judge his reaction? *Probably because you embarrassed her. Yep, that was probably it. She was being obnoxious until she found out you were a cop.* Jerry nodded his consent.

"Okay, good. Now, remember, we don't want to alarm any of the other passengers, so please stay in your seat until everyone else is off the plane."

Jerry nodded once more. "Understood."

The flight attendant stood and bobbed her head to someone Jerry couldn't see.

Houdini gave a sharp bark. Jerry placed his hand back over the top of the crate, and yet the woman in the seat next to him continued to stare straight ahead. Jerry almost felt the need to apologize to the woman. Obviously, he'd scared her by flashing his badge. Then again, if he were nice to her, she might feel the need to have an actual conversation, something he was not the least bit interested in. *No need to play nice now, McNeal. You're almost on the ground.* He smiled. *Nothing to do but grab my bags, find my ride, and head north.* A blanket of white flittered through his mind. A woman screamed. He started to reach for his gun when he realized the scream was in his head. *Another vision!* Different than any he'd had before, but definitely a vision. Jerry stretched his hands over his head. When he did, the woman next to him jumped. He started to apologize for scaring her when the plane touched down on the runway. *Just let it go, McNeal.* Jerry powered up his phone, listening as it and dozens of others on the plane went off like pinball machines.

The woman was unbuckled and reaching for her bag the second the "fasten seatbelt" sign turned off. Instead of returning to her seat, she stood, waiting to be let off the plane. Gunter took advantage of her absence, appearing in her vacant seat.

"Welcome back," Jerry whispered.

Gunter looked at him as if to say, *What do you mean? I've been here the whole time.*

"Keep an eye on the kid here. I'm going to have to take care of a situation in the back of the plane."

Gunter growled.

"I think you're right. Something is definitely off."

Jerry heard a giggle and looked to see the two little girls standing in the aisle. He shrugged. "Just talking to the puppy to keep him calm."

"It's okay," the older of the two said. "I talk to my bunny all the time."

Jerry smiled, thankful the girls could exit the plane blissfully unaware of anything amiss. Jerry slipped into the aisle seat and peeked around the chair to make sure all the passengers had departed. Satisfied, he stood and scanned the rear of the plane looking for the disruptive party. He didn't see anyone. Okay, so where'd they put him? Jerry stepped into the aisle, thinking to go have a look, when Gunter growled a deep warning. Jerry turned toward the entrance to the plane and saw two men wearing dark suits standing between him and the entrance to the cockpit.

Jerry sighed. So much for him detaining the man until help arrived. Help was already here. One of the men stepped aside, allowing a man in blue jeans and a lined windbreaker jacket to step forward. While the other two men reminded him of Fred and Barney, this guy seemed to be more of a takedown man. The trio suddenly reminded him of men walking their dog, only this dog wasn't on a leash, and instead of looking to the back where the trouble lay, he had his sights on Jerry. Gunter must have keyed on the man's intentions, as he'd slipped out of the chair and was now standing between Jerry and the federal officer.

No wonder he hadn't seen anyone in the back of the plane. The story was a lie made up to keep him on board. Jerry held up his hands. "I'm not sure what is going on, but I suggest you stop right there."

The man stopped and placed a hand on the hilt of his gun. "Yeah, and why is that?"

*Because my partner is prepared to take you down if you don't.* Jerry kept that thought to himself, knowing it would only cause them to think him delusional. Jerry concentrated on Gunter, hoping he could hear his thoughts. *Easy, boy, these men are our friends.* Jerry looked at the men. "I'm pretty sure we are on the same team. I have a badge to prove it. I don't know what you think is going on, but I'm sure whatever it is can be fixed with a simple phone call to my boss."

The man in front raised an eyebrow. "Your boss got a name?"

Jerry smiled. "Doesn't everyone? Wow, tough crowd," Jerry said when none of the three smiled. "His name is Fred Jefferies."

The man in front stood down. "You're McNeal?"

Jerry nodded. "Yep."

One of the men that had arrived first took out a cell phone. "Mystic acquired."

*Mystic?* Jerry looked at the man with the phone. "Is that Fred?"

The man gave a nod.

Jerry rocked back on his heels. "You tell him if this is his idea of a joke, I don't find it amusing. Tell him your boy here was dangerously close to being dropped in the passageway."

The man in question chuckled. "You think you could outrun a gun?"

Jerry shook his head. "Nope, but my dog can."

Houdini took that precise moment to make his appearance. Scrambling between Gunter's legs, the pup squared off, matching Gunter's stance as he imitated his father's warning.

Each of the men looked at the pup and laughed.

Jerry sighed as he reached around Gunter and scooped up the feisty pup. "He might not look like much, but I assure you, if you had come at me, you would have thought you were dealing with a much larger dog."

The men chuckled once more.

Jerry focused on the man who'd made the call to Fred. "I'd appreciate it if someone could fill me in on what just happened here."

The man who'd made the call to Fred spoke up. "The pilot radioed in that there was a situation on the plane. It was said there was a man impersonating a police officer threatening a woman on the flight. The woman slipped the flight attendant a note saying she feared for her safety and further stated she thought you were a human trafficker. Said you'd produced a fake badge and dared her to tell anyone. She thought you were planning to kidnap her the moment she got off the plane."

"And you guys just happened to be in the neighborhood?"

"I'm Monroe. This is my partner, Tyson. We were on the plane that delivered your ride."

Jerry frowned. "My Durango has a security detail?"

The man laughed. "We were on the way home from working something else and got word to get the SUV to Nashville. We were told it was a stat delivery. Figured it must belong to someone special since they were willing to take a chance on getting bogged down by the weather."

Jerry ignored the comment. "The woman is off her rocker. There wasn't anything wrong with the badge, and I didn't threaten her. She took issue with me from the start, and it escalated when she found out we were sharing a row. She threatened to have me arrested. I was tired of her crap, so I showed her my badge."

"What'd she say?"

"Nothing. I thought I had gotten through to her because she behaved like a model citizen afterward. Seriously, we never said another word to each other." Jerry ran a hand over his head. "I can tell you

I wouldn't mind having a chat with her now."

"They escorted Miss Smith directly to the airport security office when she left the plane. Your boss said they would keep her there under the guise of protective custody until we have this figured out. We have orders to escort you out."

"Out?"

"To pick up your ride. Mr. Jefferies told us we are not to leave your side until you depart the airport. If you're ready, we can take you to your vehicle." Monroe smiled. "We have to pass airport security on the way."

Jerry matched his smile. "Lead the way."

\*\*\*

Rebecca Smith was sitting at the desk chatting with an airport security officer when Agent Monroe led Jerry into the security office with his hands behind his back. Jerry narrowed his eyes at her.

Smith swallowed. "You're arresting him?"

"We can't go letting someone get away with human trafficking," Monroe said and pushed Jerry into a chair a couple of feet away from the woman. He sat the puppy crate next to Jerry's chair. "Probably have to take the mutt to the shelter."

Smith's eyes darted toward the crate, but she didn't say anything.

Monroe looked at the security officer. "I need you to sign some forms. If you'll step into the hall, my partner will go over the allegation with you."

The man looked at Jerry and frowned. "What about him?"

"He's restrained." Monroe smiled at Smith. "We'll be just outside the door. This guy tries anything, scream."

Smith glanced at Jerry and nodded her head.

Jerry waited for the door to close. "You've got to tell them you're lying."

"How come they arrested you? Didn't you show them your badge?"

"Of course I did. You told them it was fake. They have to act on threats. Why'd you tell them I threatened to kidnap and beat you?"

Her eyes grew wide. "I never said that."

"You didn't tell them I threatened to kidnap you?"

She squirmed in her seat. "I never said you were going to beat me. I don't know why they told you that."

"That part won't matter anyway because it never happened. But kidnapping and trafficking charges are serious accusations. Those could get me sent away for the rest of my life. Why, I may never see my daughter again." Jerry thought about what he'd said to the woman during their original meeting. "I was on my way home to yell at my nephew for being a deadbeat dad, and now look at me. I'll be in prison and never get to see my daughter grow up. Heck, she won't even get the puppy I was bringing home for her birthday this week. Poor little guy, they will send him to the pound."

"I didn't know I would get you in this much trouble."

"You lied. What did you think would happen?"

"I thought they'd let you go when you showed them your badge."

"But they didn't, and now I will be going to prison because… why'd you lie?"

"I don't know. You looked so smug when you showed me your badge. It kind of made me mad. Then it just came to me. I didn't know they'd send you to prison. Sorry about that."

"What do you mean sorry about that? You're going to tell them the truth."

"No. I don't think I can." There was not even a hint of remorse in her voice.

Instantly, Jerry knew this wasn't the first time she'd falsely accused someone of something. "You've done this before."

She considered this. "What if I have?"

Jerry worked to keep his anger under wraps. "So, you'd let me go to prison just because you don't want to get in trouble?"

She shrugged. "I don't know you."

"You don't know me! That's why you didn't look at me when the flight attendant asked me for help. You didn't want this to be personal."

"If I knew you, that would be different. But I

don't, so I will never have to see you again."

"What exactly is it you get from this?"

She smirked. "I like the way people look at me. Only you didn't. Not that first time. You looked at me like... like you had a secret that you weren't willing to share."

Jerry pulled his hands from behind his back.

Rebecca blinked her surprise. "I thought you were handcuffed."

"Your reign of destroying lives is over." Jerry placed his cell phone to his ear. "You'd better get in here before I do something I'll regret."

The door opened. Monroe entered, followed by his partner and the third guy who'd boarded the plane with them.

Jerry ended the call. "Did you get all of that?"

"Loud and clear," Monroe said, turning to the third man. "Get her out of my sight."

"That's not the first time she's pulled something like this," Jerry said the minute she was gone.

Monroe looked toward the door. "You sure about that?"

Jerry nodded. "Never been more sure of anything in my life."

# Chapter Nine

The cargo plane that had delivered Jerry's ride was parked just outside the hangar housing his ride. The snow swirled around the building as Jerry bid farewell to the agents who were hoping to get in the air before their plane was grounded.

Once away from the vehicle, he sat the puppy down, waited for him to empty his bladder, then walked to the airplane hangar. Houdini followed Gunter into the building, trailing his leash behind. The hangar was dark, except for red and blue lights that flashed in the middle.

Jerry walked toward the display. As he did, he found himself instantly transported back in time, watching the television show *Knight Rider*, showcasing Michael Knight's Pontiac Trans Am.

Kitt was brilliant black, with deep tinted windows and lights under the hood. Most people who watched the show dreamed of owning that car. The image cleared, but the vehicle that had prompted the vision remained. Dropping his bags, Jerry walked toward the Durango, which sat idling in the darkened hangar. While he had always been a fan of his ride, the jet-black beast sitting in front of him now looked somewhat otherworldly with the police lights flashing from within the grill, the blower vent on the hood, and near the top edge of the front windshield. Aside from the lights, everything from the newly installed grill guard to the heavily tinted windows was black. Jerry's heart rate increased. Never in his life had he seen anything even close to being this sexy, and it was his.

He emitted a nervous giggle. "So much for low profile."

Gunter alerted. A second later, the hangar's lights came on. Houdini raced to Gunter's side, ears forward and tail up, matching his father's stance while emitting puppyish woofs.

Jerry turned to see a man walking toward them.

Wearing jeans, a button-up white shirt, and sporting dark-rimmed glasses, the man moved toward him with long, confident strides. Oblivious of Gunter and ignoring the pup's warning, he reached out a hand. "Tim Grimm."

Jerry shook his hand and turned his attention

back to his ride. "This your work?"

Grimm grinned. "Sure is. Do you like it?"

Jerry raised a brow. "So, you're the agency's equivalent of Q?"

Grimm laughed. "Sort of. Only I don't have a cool name or the luxury of using Hollywood special effects in my design."

Houdini inched closer, took hold of the man's shoelace, and pulled. The string released, sending the pup backward. Not to be deterred, Houdini took hold a second time, growling as he tried to pull it from Grimm's shoe.

Jerry looked at Gunter. *Could you please control your son?*

Gunter barked and raced to the other side of the building. Houdini let go of the string and raced off, eager to join this new game.

Grimm looked after him. "You might want to catch him before he makes his way outside. He gets lost in the snow or makes his way onto the tarmac, and he's a goner."

"He's smart enough to stay inside." Even as he said the words, Jerry debated their validity. While he didn't fully trust the pup, he did trust Gunter, who'd lowered to the concrete and was now holding the end of the puppy's leash in his mouth. Jerry opened the door and climbed behind the wheel. As he scanned the newly installed computer and high-tech dashboard, he moved his hand across his mouth to ensure he wasn't drooling. "Does he talk?"

"The Durango? To the point that computers can answer you, yes. It can't carry on a conversation, if that is what you are asking." Grimm winked. "I'm a big fan of *Knight Rider* myself. Run your hand under the dash just to the right of the steering wheel."

Jerry did as Grimm said, smiling when he felt the pistol. Jerry pulled it free from its cradle, inspected it, and returned it. "Nice."

Grimm pointed to the overhead console. "Hit the button for the sunroof."

Jerry pressed the button and sucked in a breath as the cover slid back, exposing a mini arsenal capable of starting a small war. He blew out a long whistle. "I have to tell you, Grimm, I really like your style."

Grimm bobbed his head. "Thanks. If you ask me, sunroofs are highly overrated. Your windows are bulletproof, as are the doors. The bullets might scratch the paint, but they won't penetrate the reinforced steel."

Jerry started to tell the man he wasn't in the habit of getting shot at, but he'd never planned on working for a government agency without a name either, and yet here he was. "What's with the cowcatcher on the front?"

"It protects the grill from anything you might encounter. Mr. Jefferies said you do a lot of driving, so I thought it might come in handy. It's also sturdy enough to push anything out of your way if you find yourself blocked in. There's a winch in the HD bumper." Grimm pointed to the hood. "I took the liberty of doing some tweaks to the engine."

Jerry looked over the steering wheel. "Tweaks?"

Grimm waggled his brows. "It goes fast."

"It already went fast."

"We both know this is not the same Durango." Grimm's smile broadened. "This one goes really fast."

Jerry nodded his understanding. "Anything else I should know?"

"You find a button you don't know what it is, test it out. If you have any questions, let me know." He held up a finger and pointed to three buttons. "The first button is a direct line to Mr. Jefferies. You don't even need your cell phone. Your SUV is now equipped with a satellite, so you'll never be without service."

Jerry started to tell him he was hooked into the angel network and always had service anyway, but decided against it.

"That red button in the middle is your phone-a-friend button."

"Phone-a-friend?"

"You push that, it better be an emergency. Any agency nearby will be alerted that you need assistance. Which leads me to my next point."

"Dare I ask?"

"I've installed a tracking device. Nothing we couldn't do anyway, but now the agency will know where you are at all times. Have you ever used the airplane app?"

"Airplane app?"

"Yeah, it's pretty cool. You can track a flight all the way across the country. It's that way with your Durango. That radio will allow you to monitor police channels. In addition to the lights, you also have a siren, and the radio will allow you to broadcast outside your vehicle just like in a police cruiser."

Jerry smiled. "Providing that cruiser was on steroids."

Grimm stepped back and pushed a button on the key fob to open the cargo hatch. Jerry followed him to the back and looked inside to see a utility box that stretched the width of the cargo space. The third-row bench seats were folded, as was one of the middle chairs. A large dog crate sat in the middle and was lined with waterproof pads.

"The dog crate was Fred's idea. You've also got a survival trunk. You've got everything needed to sustain you and two others for at least a month." Grimm met Jerry's gaze. "I took the liberty of adding some snowshoes and tire chains. Everything is self-explanatory. Check it out and familiarize yourself when you have time. Okay, pull this, and you've got an extra room."

"Extra room?"

"Yep." Grimm waved his hand. "Turns the whole back of this thing into a camper."

"Sweet."

Grimm pushed his glasses up with his finger and handed Jerry a card. "I'm always open to suggestions if you can think of anything else."

Grimm's cell rang. "Yep? On my way." He pocketed his phone and looked at Jerry. "They've finished de-icing the plane. I've got to go before they change their minds about leaving. They told me to try and talk you out of heading north tonight."

Jerry smiled. "What, and miss trying out my spaceship?"

Grimm's face lost all humor. "It may have some cool bells and whistles, but at the end of the day, a car is only as good as its driver." Grimm pressed a piece of paper into Jerry's palm.

Jerry unfolded it. *If you ever need to go dark, press the button on the underside of the steering column.* Jerry pocketed the note and nodded his understanding.

Grimm smiled. "You be careful out there, McNeal."

"Safe travels to you too, Grimm," Jerry replied and watched as the man disappeared into the dark. Instantly, a similar vision of a man walking blindly through the snow appeared in his mind. He started to call Grimm back to warn him and then realized he was not the man in question. Jerry shook off the vision and gave a sharp whistle. "Come on, boys, time to roll!"

Gunter leapt into the front seat and then went to the passenger side. Houdini tried several times to match his father's move, then sat barking his frustration. Jerry picked him up and placed him into the back and took off the puppy's leash. He placed his seabag and travel bag on the floor on the other side and pointed a finger at Houdini. "Stay."

Houdini gave him a grumbling growl, then settled when Gunter swiveled his head around and lifted his lip.

Jerry slid behind the wheel once more and sighed a contented sigh. Even without the cool upgrades, he was pleased to have his ride back. While he'd finally made peace with his rental car, he enjoyed the space his Durango offered. Jerry waited until he'd grabbed a bite to eat and got onto I-65 before pushing the button delegated to Fred.

"I was wondering how long it would take you to call." Fred's voice boomed through the speakers. "Do you like your new ride?"

"It'll do. Where's my ride?"

"You're driving your ride. I assure you your other Durango is being well looked after."

Gunter cocked his head toward the dash. Houdini barked, then quieted.

"Is that the pup or the ghost?" Fred asked.

"That was Houdini, and technically, he's both."

"That's some life you live, McNeal." Fred chuckled. "Speaking of which, you're grounded."

"Grounded?" Jerry repeated.

"Not allowed to fly."

"I know what grounded means, but why punish me?" It wasn't that Jerry minded staying on the ground. He just didn't like to be told he couldn't do something.

Fred chuckled once more. "Don't get yourself all worked up. We're not punishing you. We are protecting you. You need to fly, we'll make the arrangements."

"In case it slipped your mind, you made these arrangements."

"Yes, I know," Fred replied. "Let's just say I don't think commercial travel suits you. Speaking of keeping your feet on the ground, are you happy with the upgrades on your SUV?"

"Most of them."

"Let me guess, Grimm told you about the tracking system I had him install."

"He did."

"Did he also slip you a note that tells you how to disable it?"

Jerry glanced at Gunter. "Maybe."

Fred laughed a hearty laugh. "Relax, McNeal. I know what it is you do. I also know there might come a time you don't want big brother watching you."

"So Grimm isn't out of a job for slipping me the note?"

"That would just be dirty pool, considering I'm the one who wrote it and told him to give it to you."

"You're a hard man to figure out, Mr. Jefferies."

"Right back at ya, McNeal. You still planning on heading north?"

"Heading that way as we speak, but you probably already know that."

"How's the weather?"

Jerry figured the man knew the answer to that as well but gave him a weather report anyway. "Looks to be about four inches on the ground. The roads are slick but drivable as long as no one does anything stupid."

"You're just getting into it. I know that ride of yours is a beast, but remember, slow and steady wins the race. Speaking of slowing down, what do you think of elephants?"

"Elephants?"

"That's right, you've been away from the news. Authorities shut down an illegal zoo in Alabama, and they are dispersing all the animals to sanctuaries across the country. The elephant is on his way to a sanctuary in Paoli, Indiana. Seems transportation was already arranged before the blizzard popped up. The place they were holding him was not adequate, and the people in charge of transportation decided to start the transfer. The truck broke down just outside of Decatur, and it took two days before they found another rig to accommodate the beast."

Jerry frowned at the dash. "Okay, I understand them wanting to move the elephant to someplace safe, but I don't understand how the agency is involved."

"Someone put his plight on social media, and it skyrocketed from there. There have been people lining overpasses and bridges across Alabama and Tennessee. It's gotten so bad, they've asked for police escorts to help them get through the major cities. It's been a real nightmare. To top it off, someone had a friend of a friend that managed to reach the president. So, now it is our problem. When I say our – I mean you."

"How exactly does escorting an elephant fit into my job description?"

"Because you're the only one we have available that is crazy enough to accept the assignment."

Jerry eyed the console. "I don't know whether to take that as a compliment or be offended."

Fred laughed. "Take it as a compliment and save us all the trouble of having you file a grievance."

"I could file a grievance?"

"You could, but it wouldn't get you anywhere."

Jerry had to give it to the man. He didn't pull any punches.

"I know you want to get to Michigan, but we

could use your help with this. It wouldn't look good if anything happened to the nation's biggest celebrity. You will be catching up with the truck shortly – we want you to stick with them. We don't expect any trouble, but just in case, we will have eyes on you the whole way. They don't want to take a chance of getting stuck in the snow, so they are staying on I-65 until they reach their exit in Indiana. You're headed that way anyway, so just think of it as a big gray wind block. Once they reach their exit, they'll have a police escort to the sanctuary, and you'll be able to add elephant escort to your resume."

At the mention of the big, gray wind block, the hairs on the back of Jerry's neck stood on end.

"You still with me, McNeal?" Fred asked after a moment.

"I'm here."

"You got quiet. You're not going to give me a hard time about following the elephant, are you?"

Jerry ran a hand over the back of his neck, debating. "You said there have been police escorts?"

"That's right."

"What about up the road?"

"Depends on the weather. What's got you spooked, McNeal?"

"Could be nothing…"

"With you, it's never nothing. Tell me what you've got."

"A gray wall."

"Excuse me?"

"It's a vision. There is a woman screaming. There's snow, lots of it, and a big gray wall. That's all I have so far, but the elephant seems to be a big piece of the puzzle."

Fred's sigh was audible. "So, we need to stop the elephant?"

An instant overwhelming feeling of doom enveloped him. Jerry shook his head. "No! I don't know what's going on, but we need it to play out."

"I'm not sure the higher-ups will like putting Tiny in harm's way."

Jerry wasn't sure what surprised him most, that the elephant's name was Tiny or Fred's admission that he wasn't the almighty. "You have a boss?"

Fred laughed. "Everyone has a boss, McNeal."

"Is he listening?"

"Nope."

"Then don't tell him."

"Her." Fred grew quiet for a moment before answering. "There are too many eyes on this. Anything happens, and we won't be able to cover it up. It will be big, messy, and public."

"In for a penny, in for a ton," Jerry replied, trying to make light of the situation. "Listen, if I get anything else, I'll let you know. Just don't change anything without consulting me. My instincts tell me if we interfere with this transfer, someone will die.

Maybe more than one someone."

"Okay, McNeal," Fred relented. "You're the expert. You need anything, you call."

"Will do."

"Hey, if you get a chance, listen to the comedy CD I left in your player. The guy's name is Mike Armstrong. He's a retired cop. I think the two of you have a lot in common."

The dash lit up, showing the call had ended.

Jerry looked over at Gunter. "Does that mean Fred thinks I'm funny?"

Gunter yawned a squeaky yawn.

"Yeah, he probably just meant the cop thing." Jerry shrugged. "Anyway, let's hope this assignment turns out to be nothing and we end up being highly paid babysitters."

Gunter gave him a look that said, *Yeah, you keep telling yourself that.*

# Chapter Ten

Even with the sloppy road conditions, it didn't take long for Jerry to catch up with the elephant. Tiny was housed in a massive steel gray crate that sat on the back of a flatbed and now loomed in front of Jerry, giving the impression he was following a large gray wall. Any doubt Jerry had about the elephant being part of his vision dissipated.

Jerry glanced in the mirror, switched to the left lane, and pulled alongside the semi, which was so covered in snow that it was hard to tell if it was deep blue or black. Lit up like a Christmas tree, the cab was one of those bus-length rigs with an extended sleeper, which he knew was set up like a mini-apartment.

Jerry peered up at the driver, didn't see or feel

anything amiss, then dropped back and fell in behind the truck where the spray coming from the tires splattered his windshield, making it nearly impossible to see. Jerry eased off the gas, lowering his speed until the truck gained some distance and visibility improved. A car slipped in between the Durango and the truck.

Jerry studied the car. "Are you trying for a picture or just stupid?" He got his answer a moment later when the car moved back into the left lane and paused, pacing the truck. Jerry saw a flash from within the car, and the driver of the semi tapped the brakes, slowing as the car sped on.

Jerry rolled his neck. "Whose bright idea was it to move an elephant during a snowstorm anyway?" Jerry closed the gap a little to discourage anyone from cutting between them and fiddled with the wipers to produce fluid to brush the snow and sludge from the windshield. He reached a finger to turn on the radio, changed the mode and pushed play. Jerry settled into his seat as the CD sprang to life, laughing out loud as the comedian poked fun at himself and others and recounted exploits from his time on the job. As he told story after story, Jerry couldn't help putting himself in the man's place and nodding his head. *Oh, what I wouldn't give to have thought of some of these.*

"Where's a cop when you need one?" Jerry said aloud when a car sped around both him and the semi at a speed much too fast for the driving conditions. Once clear of the truck, the car slowed to cut across the center pull-through reserved for authorized vehicles. Jerry started to turn on the PA system and thought better of it. The last thing he wanted to do was startle the driver of the truck. He lowered the window and yelled, summoning the phrase said by the comedian only moments before. "I authorize you!"

Gunter groaned.

Jerry powered up the window and glanced at the dog, who now looked at him as if begging him not to quit his day job.

"Fine, I'll leave the comedy to the professionals," Jerry said, brushing the snow from the door and using the button on the steering wheel to turn up the volume.

***

Had it not been snowing sideways and Jerry not following a semi at what felt at times to be a snail's pace, he would be well into Indiana by now. As it was, he was now five hours into what should have been a four-hour escort, and had not even reached Louisville. Jerry had listened to the comedy CD twice and was now listening to Joe Bonamassa and trying not to think of his bladder, which had been screaming for relief for the last hundred miles. An SUV moved up beside him, aiming a cell phone in his direction, then increased the speed slightly, pacing the truck for several moments. Jerry knew the driver was videotaping the procession. The SUV swerved, lost traction then slid into the center median. Jerry rolled his neck. The roads were getting worse, and people were getting stupider. An overpass loomed in the distance, and Jerry could see people standing on the road. Something blew in the wind. As they grew closer, Jerry could tell it was a sheet. Flapping against the wind, the message was unreadable. The semi passed under the overpass. Just as the cargo crate carrying the elephant started under, the people holding the sheet let go. The sheet sailed over the top of the box and floated toward Jerry's windshield. Catching the wind, it floated off into the field. Jerry looked at Gunter. "People have lost their collective minds."

Gunter barked.

Jerry took that as a sign that the dog agreed with him. Jerry squirmed in his seat and drummed his fingers on the steering wheel, staring at the back of the truck. "Don't you guys ever take a break?"

Houdini whimpered.

"If you have to go, use the pads. I don't want to find out you've soiled the upholstery." *Hmm, I wonder how absorbent those pads are?* He glanced at Gunter.

The dog groaned.

Jerry knew the groan would have been followed by an eye roll if it were possible. He sighed. "Yeah, probably not a good idea."

Jerry eased to the right, testing the shoulder. *No joy, the emergency lane hasn't been scraped. Four-wheel drive or not, that's a lot of snow. If I get stuck, I could be looking at hours or maybe even days before someone pulls me out.* Jerry returned to his position behind the truck. *Maybe I should just sneak off at the next exit and then catch up. That would work in theory, but what if I'm not able to catch up? Okay, probably not an issue now that I have lights, as people will move out of my way. Yeah, but they won't be of help if the on-ramp is blocked.* Jerry laughed a hearty laugh. *Fred, you know that elephant I was babysitting for you. Yeah, well, I lost him. Okay, so what's to be done? Think, McNeal. Maybe I can get the truck to stop when I do. At least if we're stuck, we'd be stuck in the same place. I wonder if Fred has the number for the men in the truck.* Jerry lifted his finger and hovered it over the button that would connect him to Fred. He eyed the third button. "First button is for Fred. The red button is for help. What about the third button?" Jerry glanced at Gunter. "Do you remember Grimm saying anything about the third button?"

Gunter jumped, placing his front paws on the dash, and nosed at the button.

"Don't do that. It's probably an ejection seat or something."

Gunter tilted his head as if saying, *You're*

*kidding, right?*

"Fine, but if you get thrown out, I'm not stopping!" Jerry hovered his finger over the button. *Come on, McNeal, where's your sense of adventure? Worst case, you get thrown out of the vehicle. At least it'll take your mind off the fact you had a large iced tea with dinner.*

Gunter barked.

"Fine, I'll do it." Jerry pushed the button. The dashboard lit up, showing an outgoing call to Mother Hen.

"Hello, Jerry?"

*April? Good ole Fred. Savannah and June don't have anything on him when it comes to matchmaking.* "April? Did I wake you?"

"No. I'm just sitting here watching television with Max."

Jerry knew she said that so he wouldn't mention the puppy. He took a deep breath, temporarily blocking Max from finding out about the puppy but purposely leaving her access to the rest so she could read him. "Tell her hello for me."

"Tell her yourself. You're on speaker."

"Hey, Max, how's it going?"

"Okay. Mom said you were coming to see me for my birthday, but I guess that's not happening now."

"What do you mean it's not happening? I happen to be on my way as we speak." She grew quiet, and he knew her to be reading him.

"No fair, you blocked me!"

Jerry laughed. "No, I just blocked you from knowing about your gift. The rest of my mind is fair game." Max was good. If he were heading toward trouble, she'd pick up on it.

"You're not calling from the plane, are you?" April's tone held a bite.

Jerry remembered their last conversation and shook his head. "No, the closest flight I could get was Nashville."

"Nashville? That's like twelve hours from here."

"Ten and a half, in good weather."

"Uh huh, and how many in a blizzard?"

*Thirty.* Jerry kept that to himself. "We are creeping along."

"We?" April asked.

"Oh, my goodness. Jerry, why do I see you with an elephant?" Max exclaimed.

"An elephant? That better be some kind of joke. That's not what we agreed on," April said.

"Wait, how come I can't read Mom either?"

Jerry chuckled. "Because I told your mom to block you from knowing what you're getting."

"What's the fun in that?" Max grumbled.

"It's called a surprise, Max. Most people enjoy them. You're a kid. Take time to enjoy the little things."

"Yeah, well, I'm only going to be a kid for a couple more days. Then I'll be thirteen."

"Maybe I should take your present back and get you a more mature gift," Jerry teased.

Gunter barked, letting him know he wasn't amused.

"Hi, Gunter," Max sang out through the speakers.

"Gunter doesn't think I should return your present."

"You didn't get me a baby gift, did you, Jerry?"

"We," Jerry corrected. "The present is from the three of us. Your mother picked it out, and Gunter and I are in charge of getting it to you safely."

"Safely? Does that mean it will break if I drop it?"

Jerry thought about that. "Yes, I believe it would. What do you think, Gunter?"

Gunter barked a single woof.

"Yep, Gunter agrees. You should never drop it."

"Okay, so it will break. How big is it?"

"That's the best part. It changes sizes."

"Like an accordion?"

"I think it makes just as much noise as one," Jerry told her.

Max laughed. "I doubt that. Mom wouldn't let me have it in the house."

"Then take it outside to play with it." Jerry enjoyed chatting with Max and April. It made the time pass quicker.

"Play with it? I'm getting too big for toys. I'll be

driving in three more years."

"That's enough of this game," April said. "If I start thinking about you driving, I'll never get to sleep tonight. So, Jerry, where are you now?" April asked.

"Kentucky. Close to where Savannah and Alex live. I'll be heading into Louisville soon." Soon being relative, since the truck in front of him had now slowed to just over thirty miles an hour.

Max gasped. "You do have an elephant. It's Tiny!"

"Max, this elephant is a lot of things, but he is not Tiny."

April chimed in. "Wait? You're helping with Tiny? You've got to get a picture of him! We've been watching them move him across country for the last two days."

"I haven't actually seen him, but I know he's in the crate. Fred told me he has a big following."

"That's putting it lightly. Why, this is bigger news than the royal wedding. Every news station is covering it. They've had specials about how they are transporting him without him freezing and how much hay he will eat on the way. The sanctuary he is going to looks amazing. They are planning on integrating him into their elephant herd. I sure hope that works. The news said he's spent most of his life living in a half-acre yard. It would be super cool to see him running free with other elephants. They rent cabins, and they have all kinds of hiking and activities plus a safari with giraffes and bears. I told Max we would take a drive down there in the spring and spend the night in one of the cabins. I wish we could have been there to greet him, but we would never get near the place. Not with the blizzard. It's got to be bad if they flew Jim Cantore to Indiana."

"Who?"

"Jim Cantore, the weatherman that covers all the storms. Ask your mom. I'm sure she knows who he is. Did you know elephants love the snow?"

He didn't, and until this moment, he hadn't cared, but hearing the excitement in April's voice was invigorating. Truthfully, he couldn't recall a conversation he'd enjoyed more.

"They've had news reporters at several zoos getting footage of elephants playing in it. The dude's a real celebrity."

"The weatherman?"

"Him too, but I was talking about Tiny. Jerry, are you driving your Durango?"

"Yes, I got it back this afternoon. It was waiting for me at the airport." Jerry was just getting ready to tell her about all the upgrades when April's words stopped him.

"You're on the news."

"What do you mean I'm on the news?"

"It just showed the truck with Tiny on it going under an overpass, and it clearly shows  a Durango following it. Someone on the overpass tossed a sheet over the side. My gosh, Jerry, if that had covered your windshield, you would have been in trouble. Anyway, a cop was there and saw the whole thing. They arrested them and are now imploring others to go home and stop putting people's lives in danger. If we weren't on the phone, I wouldn't have thought it was you because you are supposed to be on a plane. At least that's what you told me," April said sourly. "Yep, I just hit the replay on our last conversation. You said not to worry about you driving in the blizzard because you were flying."

"I didn't lie to you. Ask Fred, he made the reservations and could only get me as far as Nashville. Since I was here, and Tiny happened to be coming through, Fred asked if I could follow the elephant to help keep him safe." As the words came out of his mouth, Jerry knew he'd been had. "I'm starting to think Fred set the whole thing up."

April made a tsking sound. "You're not accusing Uncle Fred of anything unscrupulous, are you?"

"Of course not. Uncle Fred is a saint," Jerry replied.

April laughed, and once more, Jerry knew this was the woman he wanted to spend his life with. "I love hearing you laugh." *Easy, Jerry, don't scare her away.* "Max is awfully quiet. Did she fall asleep?"

"No, I was reading you. You had a vision, didn't

you, Jerry?"

"Yes."

"Jerry, the elephant is going to help the screaming lady."

"What screaming lady?" April asked.

"It's okay, April. Let Max talk it through."

"She's sad, Jerry. But that's not why she's screaming. Can you hear her? You are almost there."

"No, Max. Tell me what you see."

"Snow. Lots of it. The woman's screaming. But she's not hurt. Wait, she's screaming again. She's in pain, and then she's not. I don't know what it means, do you?"

Traffic slowed in front of him and then came to a complete stop.

"You are almost there, Jerry. You need to help her."

"What's going on, Jerry?" April's joy was now replaced with fear.

Jerry looked at Gunter, who was now sitting in the front seat wearing his police vest. "I don't know, but it's time to go to work."

"You be careful, Jerry," April said firmly.

"Yes, ma'am. Max?"

"Yeah, Jerry?"

"Is it bad enough for me to call for help?"

"She's nodding her head, Jerry."

"Okay then. I've got to go. I will have my cell with me, but don't freak out if I don't answer. Max,

*122*

if you get anything else, let me know."

"Jerry!"

"Yes, April."

"Promise me you'll be safe."

*She does care.* Jerry smiled. "I promise."

"Wait!" Max called out before Jerry ended the call. "You have to help the man."

"What man?"

"The one lost in the snow!"

Jerry looked at the pile of snow that had accumulated on his hood just in the short time he'd been sitting there. "I've got to go." He disconnected the call, pressed the red button, and sent up a silent prayer.

# Chapter Eleven

Jerry didn't know what to expect, but he knew he wouldn't be able to accomplish anything with a bladder that felt as if it were ready to burst. He made his way to the passenger side of the SUV and opened the side door. He wasn't worried that any one of the cars behind him would see. Visibility was so low, someone could be standing five feet from him and not see. He'd just started to feel some relief when his cell phone rang. Jerry answered.

"Talk to me, McNeal. I got an alert that you pressed the red button. Tell me what's going on."

*I'm relieving myself. Okay, no need to freak him out with that bit of news.* "I don't know what's going on. Give me a few minutes to figure it out."

"You pushed the emergency button before you

found out if there is even an emergency!" Fred's voice was incredulous.

"No, I pushed the button before I found out what the emergency was," Jerry corrected.

"Cut the crap, McNeal. I need to know what happened in the moments before and after you touched that button."

"The truck in front of me stopped. I knew there was an emergency, so I pushed the button and then I got out. I'm now standing outside my truck waiting to hang up with you so that I can go assess the situation."

"Why can't you go while I'm on the phone?"

"Oh, for Pete's sake. Because I don't want to add indecent exposure to the list of things I have to put in the report." Jerry smiled at hearing his grandmother's words come out of his mouth.

"What's that supposed to mean?"

Jerry knew Fred was only trying to do his job, but that didn't make the man any less irritating at the moment. "It means I had a large iced tea with dinner, and I am so dedicated to my job that I have not seen fit to empty my bladder in the last four hours, as I didn't want to take a chance of losing sight of the precious cargo I'm supposed to be protecting. I'm standing outside in a blizzard without a coat with my pants unzipped. Now, if you will let me go before I turn into a popsicle, I will assess the situation and give you a call."

"Just one question, McNeal. You've already said you don't know what's going on, so what would prompt you to hit the SOS button before finding out?"

"Because I was on the phone with Max and April when the truck stopped," Jerry said, thinking that would explain it.

"And?"

"And Max told me to make the call. I was already hitting on something, and she confirmed it."

"Confirmed it how?" Fred's voice was calmer now. "What else did she say?"

"There is a woman screaming. She's in pain but not hurt."

"Someone threatening her maybe?"

"Maybe." Even as he said it, he didn't believe it. "She said something else."

"Which was?"

*Great. I'm freezing to death, and Fred wants to play twenty questions.* "She said I have to find the man that's lost in the snow."

"From what I've seen on the weather reports, that doesn't sound promising."

"Neither does losing a certain appendage to frostbite. I'll call you when I know what we're up against," Jerry said, disconnecting the call.

Gunter was waiting for him at the back of the SUV. Jerry lifted the back gate and opened the lid to the survival box. He pulled out the first aid kit, some

126

hand heaters, an emergency blanket, two flashlights and half a dozen road flares before closing the gate and making his way to the side door. Jerry opened the door, dumped the items he'd gathered on the floor and shook his head. Houdini lay in the middle, chewing on one of his tennis shoes. "I guess I know why you've been so quiet."

The pup wagged his tail and continued to chew on the shoe.

Jerry glanced at the crate and saw several wet spots on the pee pads. *Pick your battles, McNeal. It's easier to buy new shoes than replace the upholstery.* Jerry placed both Houdini and the shoe inside the cage and rooted in his sea bag for his heavy coat. He put it on, grateful he'd kept it when leaving Pennsylvania. He pulled on his watch cap, fished out his gloves, emptied his backpack, and shoved in the supplies he'd gathered from the back. He hoisted the bag onto his back as he debated his next move.

Jerry started toward the semi hauling the elephant and thought better of it. *Come on, McNeal, best to get things under control before jumping into the unknown.* He hurried to the car idling behind him and knocked on the window. The driver powered it down two inches. Jerry flashed his badge, and the window lowered further.

A round-faced woman who looked to be in her early thirties stared up at him without blinking.

Jerry searched the car and saw she was alone.

"Do you know how to use a road flare?"

The woman shook her head. "I'm afraid not, but I could learn."

"You got snow boots and a heavy coat?"

"Yes."

"Okay, take the flares and knock on the windows of those cars until you find someone who does. Tell them to go back a distance to give drivers heading this way time to stop so they don't plow into the backs of the cars and cause a pileup. While they are doing that, knock on all the windows and tell everyone to stay inside their cars and turn on their emergency flashers." Jerry hated telling them to stay inside their cars, but there was no place safe to have them congregate. Besides, with the roads the way they were, it was highly unlikely anyone was driving fast enough to cause a major pileup.

The woman raised an eyebrow. "You're the cop. Why can't you do it?"

"Because I'm not very good at my job." The line was borrowed from Mike Armstrong's comedy tape, though in retrospect, it didn't feel as funny as when he'd heard the comedian say it. *Must be in the delivery.* "Listen, I'm going to see what's going on in front of us. I need your help to make sure we don't have a pileup behind us."

She glanced at the first aid bag. "Is that what you think is wrong?"

*Come on, lady, just do what I asked.* He shoved

some flares through the window. "I don't know. That's what I'm going to find out."

She called to him as he was turning away. "I'm an ER nurse."

Jerry instantly regretted his tone. "I'm sorry."

"No, don't be. I totally understand. I've got a first aid kit in my car. I'll find someone to use these and then come find you," she said, exiting her car.

Jerry dug into the backpack, fished out a flashlight, and handed it to her. "Okay, but use this and stay in the center of the road."

She frowned.

"The emergency lanes haven't been cleared. If you try to make your way up the outside, you could slip in a snowbank, and no one would know. Stay in the center where you can be seen."

She nodded her understanding and set out toward the small line of cars.

Jerry turned in the opposite direction setting his sights on the truck hauling the elephant.

Gunter barked and looked toward the Durango.

Jerry followed his gaze. "What?"

Gunter barked a second time and pawed at the passenger side door.

Jerry walked to the SUV and opened the door to see Houdini had freed himself from the crate and was staring up at him. Houdini barked a puppyish greeting and wagged his tail. Jerry ran a hand over his head. *I don't have time for this.* He debated leaving him, then realized Gunter was right. He picked the pup up and placed him inside the front of his coat, zipping him inside. As the pup settled, Jerry locked the Durango and set out once more.

The snow was falling sideways from the west in heavy wet flakes. Jerry listened as he walked past the steel container but didn't hear or feel any sign of distress from Tiny. He moved alongside the semi, tapped on the side of the truck with a gloved hand and watched as the window powered down.

A man with a brilliant red beard peered down at him. "We're not buying anything."

Jerry smiled. "That's good, because I'm not selling anything. You got a gun in there?"

"Look, buddy. I don't know who you are, but we know you've been following us since we left Nashville. So why don't you climb on that runner and find out," the man said evenly.

While Jerry appreciated the driver's tenacity, he'd wasted enough time. He held up his badge. "Now, if you wouldn't mind answering my question."

"My co-driver and I are both licensed to carry."

"That's not what I asked."

"Yes, sir. We are well-armed and well within our rights."

Jerry smiled. "Good enough for me. Is there a chance anyone can get near that elephant without you seeing them?"

"No, sir. We have cameras, so we can monitor him at all times. If he takes a dump, we'll know it."

"Good to know. If anyone messes with the elephant, warn them. If that doesn't work, lay on that air horn. I'm going to see what's going on up ahead." Jerry followed his own advice, walking between the cars with Gunter at his side. He'd passed three sets of cars when the driver of an orange jeep opened his door and eased his way out. Dressed in an insulated camo snowsuit with high boots that nearly reached his knees, the guy looked at Jerry's snow-covered pants and hiker boots and shook his head. "Anything I can do to help?"

Jerry smiled. "You sure can. Walk up and down this line and make sure every driver knows to get out every so often and make sure their tailpipe is clear of the snow. The last thing we need is people dying of asphyxiation. Find out if anyone has any extra room in case someone runs out of fuel." Jerry remembered Max's warning. "Anyone needs to go to the bathroom, tell them to do it next to the car on the passenger side. Other than that, unless they are medically trained, they are to stay in their vehicles. We don't want anyone wandering off and getting lost in this blizzard."

The man placed two fingers to his forehead and offered Jerry a two-finger salute. "You've got it, boss."

As Jerry trudged his way forward, a feeling of

urgency pulled at him, something he hadn't felt until after he'd seen to the others. His phone rang. He looked, saw it was Fred and returned it to his pocket. *I'll let you know when I know.* When he first placed the puppy inside his jacket, he did it out of frustration. Now, as he walked through the throng of cars with the wind howling and snow blowing around him, he was grateful for the added warmth. Jerry picked his way to the next car and realized that while the emergency flashers were on, the car itself wasn't running. He pushed the snow from the driver's side window. *Empty. That's odd. Maybe it ran out of gas, and the driver started walking. Is this the man from Max's warning?*

Gunter jumped up, placing his paws on the door. Gunter lowered and Jerry followed as he ran to the next car. It, too, was turned off with only the emergency flashers showing signs of life. He rounded the car, slipped and caught himself. Jerry brushed the snow from the window. *Empty. Okay, this is not an episode of the* Twilight Zone, *and it is highly improbable that both cars ran out of gas at the same time, so where are the drivers?*

Jerry shined the flashlight into the snow and continued walking, glad to have Gunter at his side as he picked his way forward. The snow cleared momentarily, and his flashlight reflected off something ahead. Jerry switched off the flashlight, hoping to get a better view. *Nothing.* He moved forward. The light hit on the reflectors once more. As he closed the distance, he realized he was looking at a big gray wall. A chill ran through him that had nothing to do with the weather as his brain filled in the blanks, and he knew the wall to be a motorhome blocking the road. *Who in the heck drives a motorhome in this kind of weather?*

The front of the motorhome was buried deep in the snowbank, while the length of it blocked the road. Not wishing to repeat his mistake with Holly, Jerry turned on his flashlight and carefully scanned the area as he approached, looking for any other vehicles. He didn't see any, nor did Gunter alert. While he knew he'd reached the scene, it didn't feel like an accident. Still, he proceeded with caution as he rounded his way around the motorhome. The wind howled. Gunter alerted, and Jerry realized it wasn't the wind. He hurried toward the camper, heard another scream, and broke into a run as Gunter dashed forward. Jerry slowed as he reached the motorhome. Drawing his pistol, he moved toward the door, started to identify himself as a police officer, and hesitated. I'm not a cop, and the agency I work for doesn't exist. *Who am I, and when did I lose my identity?* His cell rang. Jerry ignored it.

The door to the motorhome opened, and a middle-aged woman with purple streaks in her hair stared down the barrel of his gun. She blinked, and tears trickled down her cheeks. "Please tell me you don't intend on using that."

Gunter appeared behind the woman. The fact that the dog wasn't wearing his police vest let Jerry know there was no threat inside. He lowered his gun and flashed his badge. "Officer Jerry McNeal. How can I be of service, ma'am?"

The trickle turned into a faucet. Before the woman could answer, someone behind her screamed.

# Chapter Twelve

Jerry pushed his way around the woman and took in the scene. The screams came from a pregnant woman lying on the couch in the living room. Pulled into a fetal position and clutching her stomach, the woman was obviously close to giving birth. A girl with long black hair who looked to be in her late teens sat on a chair with her arms wrapped tightly around two younger lighter-haired girls. They stared at him with tear-filled eyes, silently pleading for him to do something.

Between the screaming and the tears, Jerry's first instinct was to run from the motorhome without looking back. Luckily for everyone, his training took over, and he stayed rooted in place. Jerry searched out the woman who had greeted him at the door. "How far along are the contractions?"

She tilted her head to draw him closer. "Her contractions are twelve minutes apart, and she's two weeks away from her due date."

The hairs on the back of Jerry's head stood on end. "It's early?"

"Not by much, and the date could be off."

Houdini squirmed inside his jacket, and the woman's eyes grew round. "I believe I saw something like that in the movie *Alien*."

Jerry unzipped his coat, and the puppy's head popped free. The girls gasped. Gunter sat in front of them and barked a single bark. *Good idea.* Jerry unzipped his coat and pulled the puppy free as he walked to where the girls were sitting. He held Houdini, petting him with long strokes as the puppy did his best to wiggle free. Jerry knelt in front of the girls. "I'm Jerry. Is that your momma over there?"

The two younger girls nodded without taking their eyes off the puppy. One of the girls managed to pull her gaze away. "She's going to have a baby."

Jerry smiled. "Yes, and I'm going to have to help her, but I can't do that and watch this puppy. He likes to get in trouble and chew on things he's not supposed to. I just don't know what I should do with him while I'm busy helping your mom."

"We could watch him," the older of the two suggested. The second girl bobbed her head in agreement.

"You could? Why didn't I think of that?" Jerry

winked at the older girl as the two younger girls dropped to the floor to play with the pup.

He looked at the older girl. "What's your name?"

"Sara." Her voice shook as she nodded to the older of the two children. "This is Kay and Beth."

Jerry continued to smile and worked to keep his voice calm as he spoke. "Sara, we're going to take Mom into the bedroom and try to make her more comfortable. None of you three are to leave the motorhome without talking to me first. Understand?"

Sara nodded.

"What if the puppy has to go potty?" Beth asked.

"It's too dangerous for you to take him outside. If he pees on the floor, we will clean it up. No one goes outside, not even the puppy." Jerry cast a glance at Gunter, who stood next to him, wearing his police vest, and stared at him with a look that said, *I understand my mission.*

Jerry turned his attention to the woman who'd met him at the door. "Have you ever assisted in a birth before?"

"No."

*That was not the answer I wanted to hear.* "Have you ever given birth?"

"Yes, I have two sons."

*That helps.* "At least you know how things work."

She laughed for the first time since he showed

up. "They were C-sections."

*Crap.*

"What about you?"

"I don't have any kids, but I've assisted on three deliveries."

The woman smiled. "Lucky you."

Jerry smiled. "Lucky us. If not for that, I would have run the first time I heard her scream."

"Something tells me that's not the truth. I'm Stacie."

"Jerry McNeal."

"Yes, you told me when you got here." The woman on the couch screamed, and Stacie hurried to her side. She returned after the contraction subsided.

Jerry lowered his voice. "I've helped with three car deliveries, and while I'm no doctor, I think it's too early for screaming."

Stacie nodded. "I've been thinking the same thing."

Jerry sighed. "We should move her to the bedroom. What is your friend's name?"

"Katlyn, but she's not my friend," Stacie said, moving toward the couch. "We just met, isn't that right, Katlyn?"

Katlyn nodded and placed her arm around Jerry's neck as he lifted her from the couch. "Are the girls okay?"

That was the thing about moms. They were always worried about everyone else. He pictured

April and her fierce determination when it came to Max, and smiled. "The girls are fine. They have my puppy to keep them preoccupied."

"It wasn't like this with them. Something's wrong."

"It will be okay. Katlyn, Jerry's a pro. He's helped deliver lots of babies."

Jerry's mouth went dry. *Three. I've helped deliver three, and none of the women screamed until the end.* He plastered a smile on his face. "You're going to be just fine."

Jerry's smile was short-lived when he saw the bedroom, which was basically a bed with three walls around it. Three very close walls and definitely not a room conducive to helping deliver a baby. *Crap.* "Okay, change of plan. Grab that comforter and follow me."

The girls looked up as they entered. Sara's face paled. "Is she okay?"

"Yep, just a slight change of plans. You girls take Houdini into the bedroom and shut the door. We're going to be busy out here for a while."

Kay scooped up the puppy, and she and Beth scrambled to the other room. Sara hesitated at the door. "You might want to put some garbage bags under that blanket. I watched my dog give birth once. It made an awful mess."

This time, Gunter stayed. Probably because he knew the girls wouldn't be able to leave without being seen.

Jerry nodded and waited until Stacie found the trash bags and readied the area before kneeling and laying Katlyn on the floor. Stacie hurried to the bedroom and returned with a pillow, placing it under Katlyn's head.

There was a knock on the door, and the ER nurse came inside without waiting for an invite.

"Honey, we have company," Jerry said, watching the nurse assess the situation.

Katlyn smiled a weak smile. "Tell whoever it is to go away. I'm not really feeling up to a party."

"Oh, but we want her to stay. She's an ER nurse. Isn't that right... sorry, I didn't get your name."

"Gail," the woman said as she shrugged out of her coat and stepped to the sink to wash her hands. "How far apart are the contractions?"

"Ten...no, make that six minutes," Stacie said when Katlyn moaned.

The moan turned into a scream. Jerry looked at Gail for confirmation that something was wrong. The nod was subtle, but it was there.

"Something's wrong," Katlyn said, echoing his thoughts as soon as the contraction subsided.

"Well, for one thing, you're still fully dressed. Okay, let's get some names, so I don't have to keep saying 'hey you.'" Gail's voice was calm yet commanding.

"I'm Jerry, that's Stacie, and this here is Katlyn,"

Jerry said, pointing to each woman in turn.

Gail looked at Stacie. "I need some clean sheets and something to wrap the baby in after it is born."

"He," Katlyn said. "He's a boy. There are some baby blankets in the laundry basket near the bed.

"When are you due?" Gail asked as Stacie hurried to get the items.

"Not for another couple of weeks," Katlyn said softly. "That's why I think something's wrong. Neither of my daughters was early."

"A couple of weeks is nothing. Besides, the third one always comes early." Once again, Gail's voice was calm and reassuring.

Gunter moved close and lay next to Katlyn. He was wearing his police vest again, and that bothered Jerry.

Stacie returned with the sheets, a hand full of towels, and several baby blankets.

"Okay, Jerry, make yourself useful," Gail said, covering Katlyn with a sheet.

"Do you want me to boil water?" Jerry asked, turning his back to give them privacy.

Gail laughed. "Only if you want some tea. I was thinking of something more along the lines of calling to see how far away that ambulance is. You did call for one, didn't you?"

"It's no use," Katlyn's voice choked when she said it. "There's no cell service out here."

"She's right," Stacie said, bobbing her head.

"That's why me and Sara set our emergency hazards and turned our cars off. We thought maybe someone would see the empty cars and come looking for us. We didn't know what else to do. We couldn't get service, and there wasn't anyone else around when we saw the motorhome spin out of control."

"I got through." Jerry was happy to be able to give some good news. He realized he still had to call Fred to apprise him of the situation. "Help should be here any minute."

"Okay, Katlyn." Gail's voice was soothing. "Relax. I need to check you out to see what's going on with the baby."

Jerry's psychic radar tingled when Gunter appeared in front of him and pawed at the door. Jerry ignored his request to go outside. "Sounds like some mighty fancy driving. You must be one tough woman to drive this beast while in labor. Especially in a blinding snowstorm." Jerry left out the fact that he thought she was foolish for attempting such an act in the first place.

"I wasn't driving. My husband Joe was. My mother lives on the other side of Shepherdsville. We were going to set the motorhome up in her driveway until after the baby is born. We wanted to be closer to the hospital. I'm not due for another two weeks, so we thought we had time."

Gunter tilted his head as if to say, *That's what I've been trying to tell you.*

Jerry started to turn around, then caught himself. "Katlyn, where is your husband now?"

"I don't know." Her words came out as a sob. "When Joe couldn't get the motorhome out of the snowbank, he turned on the generator to keep us warm and left to find help."

"You can turn around now, Jerry."

Jerry turned to face them. While Gail's voice was calm, Jerry could feel her struggling to hold it together.

"I'm going to need a pair of scissors." Gail walked to the kitchen area and started opening drawers. She lowered her voice when Jerry stepped beside her. "The baby is breech. His head is turned in the wrong direction, and he's coming feet first. I'm going to have to attempt to turn him."

"Would that explain the screaming?"

She smiled and gave him a look as if to say, *You poor dumb man, bless your heart.*

He shrugged. "Is there anything I can do to help?"

Gail shook her head. "That baby's going to come with or without you here, God willing. Either way, there's nothing for you to do other than stand there and worry. But this baby's going to need a father, so you need to find Joe. He's been out in that blizzard a long time."

Jerry recalled Max's words. *You have to help the man.* He turned to look for Gunter and saw the dog standing with his head sticking out the door. "Let me call my boss and see how long before help arrives."

Gail nodded and went back to be with her patient. Jerry walked to the front of the motorhome to make the call. Fred answered even before Jerry heard the phone ring.

"McNeal! What took you so long? Why didn't you answer my call?"

"In case you forgot, I'm in the middle of a blizzard and have been a little busy," Jerry said tersely.

Fred ignored the quip. "What's the situation?"

"We've got a woman in labor and a husband who set off in the blizzard to get help. What's the ETA on getting me some assistance? I'm going to need two ambulances, a tow truck that can handle a large motorhome, and probably some gas unless everyone waiting for the interstate to open was smart enough to keep their tanks full."

"I'll relay your request, but the last time I checked, your ambulance was at least an hour out, probably even longer if things are as bad as you say. I'm afraid you're out of luck with the tow truck. You'll be lucky to get one of those by morning."

"You get me a tow truck, or I'm going to pry that elephant out of the box and hook him up to this motorhome," Jerry fumed into the phone.

"Do you think you can find him?" Fred asked, ignoring Jerry's outburst.

"I'll find him. The question is will I find him before it's too late." Jerry lowered his voice to a whisper. "Let the ambulance driver know the baby is breech. And, Fred, I'm leaving Houdini here in the motorhome with the kids. If anything happens to me, I trust you to see that he gets to Max."

"You just concentrate on saving the day. And McNeal?"

"Yeah?"

"This thing goes sideways – I'll deliver the pup myself."

Jerry looked at Gunter, and the dog smiled. Jerry couldn't decide if it was *an I'll beat you to it smile or an I'll hold him to it smile*. Either way, he had no doubt that Max would get her pup.

# Chapter Thirteen

Jerry stood outside the motorhome trying to get a bead on Joe – something he found difficult to do in a blinding snowstorm with nothing to go on except the man's first name. Even Gunter seemed to have difficulty as he'd started one way, then the other, before finally stopping and looking to Jerry for guidance. Jerry wasn't sure if it was due to the weather or because maybe the dog knew the man was no longer viable.

Jerry ran his hand over his head. "I'm not going to give up on him. Come on, Joe, talk to me, buddy." *Nothing. Wait, what was it Savannah said about using something personal to guide me?* Jerry went back inside.

Gail looked up briefly, shook her head, then

turned her attention back to her patient. Jerry turned and walked to the console looking for something he could identify as belonging to the man. He was just about to turn away when he saw a man's wristwatch hanging from the visor. Jerry picked it up and instantly received a vision of a man covered in snow. Satisfied, he headed to the door. He saw the first aid kit, started to take it, thought better of it, picked up his backpack instead, and left without a word.

Gunter was waiting for him outside. Jerry lowered the watch to the K-9, thrilled when Gunter barked and took off running north on the interstate. Jerry shoved his gloved hands in his coat pockets, lowered his head, and started after the dog, who had disappeared in the blowing snow. It didn't matter; Joe's watch was enough to provide a beacon that would help lead him to the man. Jerry just hoped he wouldn't arrive too late.

Going was slow. Without traffic to keep the snow pushed down or a wind block to keep it from blowing onto the road, Jerry found the walk treacherous. Some spots had hardly anything, and in others, he found himself trudging through snow piled nearly a foot deep. And yet, he kept walking, doing his best to ignore the chill that embraced him. *Come on, Joe, show yourself so we can both go inside and get warm.*

A dog barked. Jerry swiveled the flashlight and saw nothing. Jerry kept walking. Another bark. At first, Jerry saw nothing, and then Gunter was standing in the middle of the road without a flake of snow on him. Jerry brushed the snow from his face with his gloves. "Showoff."

Gunter barked, took off toward the east side of the road then barked, asking Jerry to follow.

Jerry shined the flashlight toward what he thought to be an open field, then trained the light on Gunter. "You've got to be kidding, right?"

Gunter barked and spun in a circle.

"Stop it. You're not Lassie, and Timmy's not stuck in the well." Jerry swallowed. "Please tell me Joe's not stuck in the well."

Gunter turned and took off over the snow without leaving as much as a paw print. Jerry followed, shining the light in front as he gingerly picked his way through the knee-high snowbank. Jerry took a step, his foot slipped, and he found himself sliding down an embankment. He reached out, trying unsuccessfully to find something to still his descent. When he came to a stop, Gunter was there, whining and licking the snow from his face. Jerry buried his face in the dog's fur. "You should have warned me about that drop-off. It was a doozy."

Gunter whined.

"Apology accepted." Jerry took inventory, thankful not only that he'd maintained his grip on his flashlight but that nothing seemed to be hurt other than his pride. On the downside, the snow had managed to work its way under his shirt, causing him to shiver uncontrollably. *Onward, Marine. Keep moving before you freeze to death*. Jerry fought his way out of the snow and continued on his way, carefully testing every step. His cell rang, reminding him he hadn't bothered to look to see if he still had it after the fall. He pulled it from his pocket, standing in place, shaking as he answered the call.

"Jerry, are you alright?" April's voice sounded troubled.

*Depends on what you'd consider being alright*. He didn't want to worry her, so he lied. "Just taking a walk in the snow."

"That's what Max just said. Only she didn't seem happy when she said it."

"It's after midnight. What is she still doing up?" Wow, had he just used the dad voice?

"She said to tell you yes, but it's okay."

She'd heard him. How? It was weird. "Wait, tell her I didn't mean that."

"Are you sure you're okay, Jerry? You sound so cold."

"I'm good." *Chill. Frozen like a popsicle*.

"Maybe I should just let you two talk."

"Jerry?"

It took him a second to realize Max was on the phone and not actually speaking to him inside his head. "I can't really talk right now, Max. I'm trying to find someone." Not only that, he didn't want them to hear him freeze to death. *Keep walking, Marine.*

"I know. You're trying to find the man in the snow."

"I am. Do you see him?"

"Yes. You need to move to the right a little. He's following the light."

"My flashlight?"

"No, the house. He saw the light. That's why he went off the road. The snow cleared, and he saw the light. Only the light went off, and now he's trying to find it again. You're cold, Jerry. I can feel it. You're going to be okay. Alex is on the way."

"Alex? Savannah's Alex? What do you mean she's on the way?" *She doesn't need to be out here. It's too cold. Oh, so cold.*

"You said you were almost to their house, so I called them."

"You need to call them back. They don't need to be out here. The roads are too bad."

"Don't be mad, Jerry. Granny told me to call them. She said you needed help. She's worried about you." Max gasped.

"What is it, Max?"

"It's the man. The light's back on, only he got turned around, and now he's heading the wrong way."

"I don't understand, Max. Isn't it a good thing that he's heading toward the house so he can be found?"

"No, it was a good thing before, but now it's not."

"Why not, Max? What's wrong with the house?"

"Nothing's wrong with the house, Jerry. It's the pond. The pond is between him and the house. The man got turned around. It's covered with snow, and he won't see it. The ice isn't strong enough, Jerry! You have to stop him. Hurry, before it's too late!"

Jerry dropped the phone into his pocket. Gunter appeared in front of him and started a slow turn to the right. Jerry followed on blind faith, running in slow motion, each step a painful reminder that he was alive. He stretched his leg as far as it would go, then pulled the other forward as if the snow were a chilled quicksand whose only mission was to keep him from completing his mission. It was a chore to breathe as the frigid air reached icy fingers deep into his lungs with each breath. "So cold. Is that a motor humming? Probably just my imagination. How much further, dog?"

Gunter barked. Then barked again and continued as if guiding him.

*You're almost there, Jerry.* The words sounded as if they belonged to someone else.

*I don't want to do this anymore. I'm so tired. Maybe if I just sit down for a moment.*

*No, Jerry. Keep going.*

Gunter …Barking so close. Jerry shined the

flashlight.

"Stop, don't come any closer!"

Jerry froze then realized the voice wasn't the one in his head. He focused the light on the voice and saw a man covered in snow. "Joe?"

"Don't come any closer. I'm on ice. I heard it crack beneath my feet. I don't think I'm too far out, but my feet are frozen. I'm not even sure my toes are still attached. I'm done for. I don't have the strength to jump."

*How am I supposed to save him when I can't even feel my own body. Come on, Marine, hold it together.* Jerry heard the hum of a motor in the distance as he eased his foot forward, and brushed it from side to side to ensure he was on solid ground before moving forward and repeating the process. He took a step and felt his foot slide. He swayed. *It would be so much easier just to allow myself to fall and be done with it.*

Gunter whined. Jerry felt something tug at his coat, pulling him back. *Gunter.*

The dog let go and proceeded to pace back and forth.

Jerry reached his arm toward Joe. "Take my hand."

Joe lifted his arm, yanking it back as a loud crack filled the air. "It's no use. I've already made peace with the fact I won't ever get to hold my son. It sucks to go out like this. I walked on hot coals on a dare from my brothers and can't summon the energy to make my legs move to get me out of this mess. I was almost there too. I saw the light from the house. I was going to get them help."

Jerry's heart thumped hard in his chest. "You're a Marine?"

Joe nodded. "Got hit with some shrapnel a few years ago and took it as a sign I should get out and spend more time with my family. I guess I was fooling myself, thinking I'd be lucky enough to have a family I could share my hopes and dreams with."

The hum of the motor grew closer. Help was on the way. He could feel it. *I've got to get him off the ice before it gives way.* "Give me your hand, Joe."

"I can't seem to move my arm. Do me a favor?"

"If I can?"

"Don't tell my family you found me like this. Let them dredge the lake and find my body. Let them remember me as a man who was trying to save them, not someone too weak to move his arms."

An image flashed of the man stepping back into the pond. A few moments ago, Jerry was ready to give up, and now anger soared through his veins. "That's it? Your wife is willing to fight for your baby, and you're just going to give up? No wonder women are the ones to give birth. If it were up to a man, there wouldn't be any kids because we'd simply give up because it's too hard."

"What do you expect me to do?"

"I expect you to fight for what you want. Just like I intend to do. Do you think I want to be out here? I was on my way to Michigan to tell the woman I love that I don't want to spend another moment without her in my life. Do you know what that's called, Joe? It's called love, and love is worth fighting for. Do you love your wife, Joe?"

"Yes."

"What about those little girls? I've got a daughter; her name's Max. I might not be her biological father, but she's the daughter of my heart. What about your daughters, Joe? Do you love them?"

"I love them all with every breath in my body." Joe's voice held conviction.

"Then let's go home to them, Joe. You go home to your wife, and I'll go home to April and Max. We're both going home to our families, you and me, right here, right now. All you have to do is grab my hand," Jerry said, extending his arm.

Jerry felt Joe's hand graze his. He tightened his fingers around Joe's wrist and yanked with everything he had. The next thing Jerry knew, he was on the ground with Joe lying on top of him. His head throbbed and felt as if something had exploded. Gunter licked his face.

*Gunter...get help.*

At first, he thought it was Gunter whimpering next to him, but then he realized the sobs belonged to Joe. Jerry wrapped his arms around the man. "Hang in there, brother. This is not your night to die."

Jerry lay there, willing his arms to find the strength to move. He was finally able to roll Joe to the side and slowly pulled himself to his knees. He slipped off the backpack, unzipped it and pulled the emergency blanket free. He tried to open the package, but his hands were trembling too much. He brought the package to his mouth and ripped it open with chattering teeth. *The wind's roaring. No, it's a motor. Or is that a dog barking? I've got a dog? I wonder whose dog that is?* The wind pulled the blanket from his hand and called him by name. *How does the wind know my name?*

"Jerry?" A light flashed in front of his eyes. "Jerry?"

"Alex?"

"That's right, Jerry. It's okay, brother. I've got you now. It's not your day to die. Don't you go to sleep on me. Savannah will never forgive me."

\*\*\*

Jerry heard voices and opened his eyes to find himself in a hospital room. He started to get up and realized his hands were strapped to the side of the bed. "Arrested?"

"You're awake?"

Jerry turned to see Alex standing by the side of his bed. "Why am I handcuffed?"

She laughed. "You're not handcuffed. They have you in restraints."

"Who'd I kill?"

Another laugh. "No one. But you did threaten to, and I quote 'beat the tar out of the doctor if she didn't give you your pants and car keys.'"

"Ouch. What did she say?"

"She ordered you a cocktail and told the nurse to let you sleep it off."

"It must have worn off. I feel like I've been run over by a truck."

Alex smiled. "Try a two-hundred-pound man."

"Joe?"

"He'll live. But he might lose a couple of his toes. Apparently, he had a hole in the sole of one of his shoes."

"Me?"

"Hypothermia and concussion."

"How did you find us?"

Alex smiled. "Gunter."

"I'll need a little more than that to fill in the blanks."

"Max called Savannah and told her you were in trouble. She said you'd told her you were close to our house. Savannah called Fred, who explained there was trouble. He knew exactly where you were, but no one could get to you. So, we – me and some friends – hopped on snowmobiles and came to find you. We were near to where the backup was when I saw Gunter. I knew if he let me see him, you must be in trouble, so I followed him. To be honest, when I got there, I thought I was too late."

"I think I remember you being there. Something about not my day to die."

Alex shrugged. "I think I recall you saying something similar to me not too long ago."

Jerry struggled to ask the question he wasn't sure he wanted to know. "How's Katlyn and the baby?"

Alex smiled. "Both mother and baby are fine. Katlyn asked me to let her know when you wake up."

"How long have I been in here?"

"A day and a half."

"A day and a half!"

Alex winked. "It was some good drugs."

Jerry had so many questions, but his head was swimming, making it hard to hold a thought. He tried to raise up, saw Gunter lying at the foot of his bed, and relaxed.

"Where do you think you're going?"

"I was looking for Gunter. He's here. Now I need to find Houdini."

"Houdini is fine. He's with Savannah."

"I've got to tell her something."

Alex smiled a wicked smile. "Fred already told her. I thought her head was going to blow off."

"Why is she mad about the puppy?"

"Boy, that concussion has you all kind of

screwed up. She's not mad about the puppy. She's mad she had to hear about it from Fred. Seriously, dude, a ghost puppy is big news! Don't worry, we've been sworn to secrecy."

"I've got to call April and Max. They have to be worried sick," Jerry said, pulling at his restraints.

The lines on Alex's face softened. "They know. You've called them three times, and they've called here at least a dozen more."

Jerry frowned. "I have?"

Alex nodded. "Hey, I've got something to show you." She turned her phone around to show a video clip of a woman sitting behind a news desk. "And in a strange twist of fate, Tiny, the rescued elephant that has captured the hearts of the nation over the last couple of weeks, became the rescuer. It all happened when the truck taking Tiny to his new home got caught up in a traffic jam during yesterday's blizzard. With no wreckers available to clear the way, Tiny was summoned into service to help dislodge a motorhome that had spun out of control and therefore wreaking havoc for motorists unlucky enough to be traveling during the blizzard. The mighty elephant seemed pleased to be out of his enclosure, and after his heroic deed was captured on video frolicking through the snow with a large German shepherd dog thought to belong to one of the people caught in the traffic jam." The video ended showing a brief clip of Gunter running through the snow as the elephant chased after him.

Alex smiled and shook her head. "You would have thought no one on the planet had seen an elephant before. People piling out of their vehicles to get pictures and video. The elephant was hesitant at first, and then Gunter showed up, and it seemed as if he were talking to him and letting Tiny know everything would be okay. Someone streamed it live. Fred was so excited to see the dog that I thought he was going to have a stroke."

Jerry smiled. *It may have been on video, but Fred finally got to see his ghost.*

# Chapter Fourteen

Jerry walked down the hospital corridor with Gunter by his side. He found the room he was looking for and hesitated.

"Jerry!" Joe said, waving him in. "You're dressed. Does that mean they sprung you, or you're leaving AMA?"

"I take it you heard about the poll?" Jerry said, speaking of the bet the nurses had made of whether he would stay in the hospital until his doctor officially discharged him.

Joe bobbed his head. "I knew you'd stay. Anyone who does what you did for me isn't a quitter."

"I thought about it a few times, but in the end, I knew my boss would object."

"Think he'd fire you?"

"No, I think he would have had someone come in and physically sit on me if I tried to leave before the doctors gave me the all-clear." Jerry had a memory of the man saying those exact words, though he wasn't sure if Fred had actually said them or if he'd just dreamt it.

"Have a seat."

"I can't stay. I need to get on the road."

"Just for a couple of minutes. The wife is on her way up with the baby. She wants you to meet him since you're the reason he is here."

Jerry shook his head. "I know my memory is foggy, but I'm pretty sure I was nowhere near when the baby was born."

"Your memory is foggy because you hit your head when I landed on you." Joe wrinkled his brow. "I can't thank you enough for what you did out there. If not for you…"

Jerry held up his hand. "No need to thank me, brother."

Gunter alerted, looking to the door while wagging his tail.

Jerry pushed from his chair as Katlyn entered the room. The change from the last time he'd seen her was remarkable. When he'd left to find Joe, she had been withering in pain and was pale, with her sweat-soaked hair plastered against her head. Now, her dark hair bounced as she walked, her eyes sparkling as she held a blanketed bundle in her arms. He smiled. "You look much better than the last time I saw you."

She raised an eyebrow. "That's all I get?"

Jerry glanced at Joe, whose belly laugh showed he'd found his wife's comment exceptionally amusing. "Am I missing something?"

Katlyn walked to the bed and bent, giving Joe a lingering kiss. She stood. "I had my mother wheel me to your room so that I could personally thank you for saving our lives. You took one look at me and proclaimed me the Madonna."

Jerry smiled. "They had me on some good drugs."

"Okay then, now that your head is clear. Thank you for saving our lives," she said, waving her hand to include herself, Joe, and the baby.

"Everyone keeps saying that. I get Joe, but you and the baby – sorry, I don't know what you named him – you two owe your thanks to Gail."

Katlyn looked at the baby as she spoke. "I don't discount what Gail did. He and I would have died if she hadn't known what to do. The cord... anyway, yes, Gail saved both of us. But she told me she would not have gotten out of her car if you hadn't approached her. There was another nurse closer to the motorhome. If someone had gone looking for help, they would have stopped at her." She lifted her gaze, staring at him as if willing him to understand. "Jerry, the woman in the other car may be a great nurse, but she has never delivered a baby."

Jerry swallowed and nodded his understanding.

"Hey, don't forget about the elephant," Joe said from his hospital bed.

A wide grin spread across Katlyn's face. "No, let's not forget about Tiny. They brought both you and Joe to the motorhome to wait for the ambulances. However, they couldn't get to us because the roads hadn't been plowed. Only the southbound lanes were clear because several plow trucks were stuck in line behind us. It was crazy with everyone talking at once and trying to figure out how to get the motorhome out of the snowbank. I'm crying on account of Gail has already told me I probably need a transfusion. The baby was blue when he came out, so we were worried about that. We thought Joe was dying. We thought you were dying. The girls were crying. Come to think of it, I even remember hearing a dog howling. Then, out of nowhere, you regain consciousness, sit up and start barking orders."

Jerry didn't recall any of what Katlyn was saying, but he did remember hearing Gunter howl and knew it was the dog that led him out of the darkness. He glanced at Gunter, and the dog offered a K-9 smile. "You said I was barking orders?"

Katlyn grinned. "Forgive me if I clean up the language. You said we didn't need to wait for a tow truck, that we have our own. You told Alex to go back there and deputize the elephant. I believe there was a slight standoff between her and the driver of the truck until your boss got involved and authorized the elephant to be removed from the truck."

*Joseph Cody McNeal.* Jerry's head snapped up at the mention of his brother's name. "Excuse me?"

Katlyn stood in front of him, holding the baby for him to see. Gunter moved close, sniffing the infant.

"I asked if you would like to meet Joseph Cody Pernell," she said, placing the infant in his arms.

As Jerry stared at the baby, he had a flash of another infant being placed in his arms. His mother hovering protectively close, proclaiming this to be his new baby brother, Joseph Cody McNeal. As Jerry held the baby, he felt the joy of a long and prosperous life. He smiled at Katlyn and handed her the child. "I like the name."

She knitted her eyebrows. "You should. You helped name him."

"I did?"

"Yes, while we were waiting for the ambulance. I told you we wanted to name him after my husband but hadn't settled on a middle name. I asked you for yours, and you said you had another name that would be better."

Jerry worked to hide his surprise. "I'm glad I suggested it. It fits him." He glanced at the clock and stood. "I'd better be on my way. My friend is meeting me downstairs with Houdini."

"That puppy is nothing short of an angel."

*Even more than you know.* Jerry glanced at Gunter. "Why's that?"

"Just the way he was able to distract the girls so they wouldn't be so scared."

Jerry shrugged. "I'm just glad we were in the right place at the right time."

Katlyn sat on the side of Joe's bed and sighed a contented sigh as he reached his arm around her. "So are we," they both said, lending to their compatibility.

Joe raised his arm and doubled his hand into a fist. "Semper Fi, brother."

Jerry repeated the gesture. "Hoorah, Marine."


Jerry left, and Gunter took his place at his left side. Jerry was grateful fate had placed them at the right place and time to see Joe and his family safe. As he walked, he thought of April. *What was it Joe had said? That he wanted someone he could share his hopes and dreams with? I want that too, only that's not all. I want someone I can talk to after a particularly rough day, tell my secrets to, and confess my fears.* Seltzer and his wife June were like that, and he'd noticed Alex and Savannah finishing each other's sentences a time or two. Jerry thought of April and longed for that which he'd yet to obtain.

\*\*\*

Savannah stood in the parking garage hugging the puppy close. "Are you sure you don't want to leave him with me and Alex?"

Jerry grinned. "I doubt that would make Cat happy."

Alex bobbed her head in agreement. "You're right. He's happy being king of the castle."

"Fine," Savannah pouted. "You tell Max to call me if she ever needs a puppy sitter."

Jerry nodded. "That I can do."

Gunter barked.

Jerry gave a nod to the dog. "Someone's feeling left out."

Savannah dropped to her knees in front of him, giving him a thorough scratch. "Yes, I love you too, big guy."

Alex shook her head. "If I didn't know better, I would say you have both lost your minds."

"But you do know better, don't you?" Savannah said with a wink.

"Yes, I do," Alex said, looking toward the dog, which she could not currently see. She lifted her eyes and saw Jerry watching. She held his stare. "I don't know how any of this works, but I'm glad that dog has your back."

"That makes two of us," Jerry replied.

Savannah handed him Houdini and gave him a fierce hug. "Drive safe." She sniffed and stepped aside to allow Alex closer.

Jerry held up a finger and reached inside the Durango. He pulled out the comedy CD. "Fred gave me this. I think you'd like it."

"You're right. Mike is great." She handed it back to him and winked. "Keep it. I already own a copy."

Jerry put the CD back and opened the back door to place Houdini in the crate. He pulled out what looked like a long, angled stone. The pup reached for it. "What's this?"

"It's a moose antler." Savannah gave him a pointed look. "It's much safer for him to chew on than a sneaker."

"Yes, Mom," Jerry said, placing both it and Houdini in the crate. He looked at the pup and held up his hand. "Stay." Houdini seemed content to do just that as he settled down and began chewing on the antler.

Jerry looked at Gunter. "Ready to roll, boy?"

Gunter barked, then jumped through to the front passenger side seat.

"McNeal?"

Jerry turned toward Alex.

"You ever want to sell that ride of yours, I get first dibs."

Savannah laughed. "She's serious. She's been going on about it ever since she drove it home the other night. You're lucky you got it back."

Jerry glanced at the sunroof.

"Don't worry," Alex called over his shoulder.

"Everything is just where you left it. But just so you know, if we ever go to war, I'm on whatever side you're on."

"Wouldn't have it any other way," Jerry said as he climbed into the driver's seat.

Once outside the garage, he looked at Gunter. "I sure do wish I had a crystal ball that would tell me what the future holds for us."

Gunter groaned and looked at him as if to say, *Please tell me you're kidding.*

*** 

For the first time in his life, Jerry was running to something and not scrambling to get away. The only anxiety he felt was that he couldn't get there fast enough. *That's a lie, McNeal, and you know it. Why don't you just admit that you are terrified – worried that you'll confess your feelings and she'll send you away.* Jerry looked at his reflection in the rearview mirror. "Stop it. Everyone deserves to be happy. Even you, McNeal."

Jerry hit the Uconnect button, searched out Seltzer's number, and hit connect.

"Jerry, are you still flying high, or have you been sprung?"

Jerry eyed the dash. "I take it I've already called you?"

"I think you called everyone you know."

"I hope I didn't say anything I'll regret."

His former boss chuckled. "Enough to make me

ask June to take away my phone if I ever find myself incapacitated. I called the nurses' station the following day and found out they'd taken your phone away so you could get some rest. The doctor told you that you were not in any shape to drive, so you told them you'd walk. When they refused to give you your pants and keys, you demanded they call me so that I could come arrest whoever stole them."

"Great," Jerry groaned.

"You told me you were going to Michigan as soon as they sprung you. Are you sure you're up for the drive? Give me the word, and I'll drive down and drive you myself."

"Already there. I'm heading up the lakeshore as we speak," Jerry informed him.

"You don't sound very happy about it."

Jerry sighed. "I'm getting ready to profess my love to a woman who may or may not turn me away on my ear."

"Why do you think she'll turn you away?"

"I don't. At least, I hope not, but there is always that possibility."

"Maybe you should've asked for some of those drugs they had you on."

"Why is that?" Jerry asked, even though he had a feeling he wasn't going to like the answer.

"You were pretty cocky. Said you'd just gotten off the phone with April and how you'd told her everything."

Jerry swallowed. "What did I say?"

"That was it. You said you'd just told her everything."

*Great. I probably made a complete fool of myself.*

"Don't do it!"

"Don't do what?"

"Turn around. That's what you're thinking, isn't it?" Seltzer chuckled. "Son, I know you as well as I know myself. Maybe you should take a page out of Manning's book."

At the mention of the name, Gunter's head popped up, his ears tilting toward the back of the seat as he stared at the dash.

"Manning? What does he have to do with anything?"

"I'm only saying that the boy is a lot of things, but he isn't afraid to make a commitment."

"You're not saying…"

"Yep. He and Linda are getting married in the spring. They want to wait until after the baby is born so he can be the ring bearer."

"Don't they have to be able to walk for that?"

Jerry heard the familiar creak of Seltzer's chair. "Apparently not. Listen, it's obvious you love the gal, and it's okay to be scared to tell her so. I can't tell you how many times I chickened out of telling June that I loved her. Just don't wait until it's too late."

"Meaning?"

"April's a good-looking gal, and you need to tell her how you feel before someone else scoops her up and steals her away."

"Do you know something I don't?"

"No, but it happens all the time. If you don't believe me, just read one of my wife's books."

Jerry laughed. "I'll pass. I'm not the police porn type."

"Suit yourself. The captain's heading this way, so I'd better go. And, McNeal?"

"Yeah, Sergeant?"

"Good luck."

"Thanks," Jerry replied, disconnecting the call.

\*\*\*

Jerry stood at the side of the Durango for several moments before scooping up the pup, stuffing him inside his coat, and heading to the house. The door opened even before he reached the front porch. Gunter raced ahead of him, eager to greet Max.

April stood to the side, her face unreadable. "Back up and let Jerry in," she said when he reached the porch.

Max scrambled backward, giggling as Gunter continued to lick her face. Jerry stepped inside, pulling the door closed behind him as Max pushed from the floor and hurried to give him a hug. "I'm so glad you're okay. We were so worried."

*We?*

Houdini squirmed.

Max let go, eyeing the continuing movement within his jacket. Before she could say anything, Houdini wiggled his head free.

Max squealed, and the head retreated inside the coat. "A puppy! I never dreamed my present would be a puppy!"

"Oh, Max, you scared him," April said, stepping forward. She held Jerry's gaze as she unzipped his coat and pulled the puppy free, handing him to Max. "Happy birthday."

Max hurried to the living room and dropped to the floor, giggling with delight as Houdini smothered her with eager puppy kisses.

April looked him up and down. "You look tired."

"It's been a long couple of days."

"So I heard."

"Seltzer told me I called you."

"You don't remember?"

"Some things are still a bit fuzzy."

"And yet you still managed to find your way here."

*All I had to do was think of you.* "I did and so did my Durango," Jerry said, speaking to the fact his original Durango was parked in April's driveway.

"Apparently, Fred thought it belonged here." April firmed her chin. "Why are you here, Mr.

McNeal?"

*Mr.?* Jerry struggled to recall his phone call with April. He found nothing. "I came to bring the puppy to Max."

"That's a long drive just to bring a puppy."

Jerry wasn't an expert at relationships, but this conversation didn't seem to be going in the right direction. *Say something, McNeal.* "What if I said I didn't just come to bring a puppy?"

"Meaning?" April pressed.

Gunter bumped into the side of his leg, leaning against him, a solid reminder letting him know anything was possible.

Max held on to the puppy and stared at him as if willing him not to blow it.

Jerry gathered his courage. "Meaning I care deeply for both you and Max."

April shook her head, letting him know that was the wrong answer. "You care for a puppy, Jerry. We need more than that."

*April was right. He didn't care for them. He needed them in his life more than he'd ever needed anything else.* He remembered the words he'd said to Joe when they both thought all was lost, and suddenly, the courage was there. "I love you, April." Jerry met her stare and spoke with more conviction. "I love you. With the exception of my mother and grandmother, I have never said those words to another woman."

She stared at him with hopeful eyes. "Are you sure, Jerry?"

"April, I have never been more sure of anything in my life."

April glanced at Max, who gave him a long look.

Jerry spoke directly to her without uttering a word. It was the way he used to speak to his grandmother and the way Max had reached him the night he'd almost given up. *I know you've both been hurt in the past, but I promise I won't let either of you down. I love you and your mother. While I am not your father, I would like to be if you will let me.*

Tears streamed down Max's face as she shook her head. "Jerry's telling the truth, Momma."

April reached for his hand and intertwined her fingers in his. "Welcome home, Jerry. You and me and Max, right here, right now."

Jerry searched his mind to recall where he'd heard those words.

April looked at Max, and when she turned back to him, her eyes were brimming with tears. "We were there with you, Jerry. You must have forgotten to turn off the phone when you put it in your pocket because we heard everything you said. I was scared when everything went quiet, but Max kept talking to you and assured me she could still feel you and knew you were alive. We believed in you and knew you would be coming home to us."

"Then why all of this?"

"Because we needed to know that you believe in us too."

Gunter lifted his head, emitting a single long howl. Houdini trotted to where his father sat and lifted his head, his howl ringing out in puppyish yips.

Gunter lowered his head and looked at the pup as if to say, *Don't worry, kid. We've got an eternity to work on that.*

# A Note from the Author

I want to thank everyone who has read this series. The response to my Jerry McNeal series has been more than I could have ever wished for. Staying in the writing chair all last year to give you a book a month has had its challenges but offered many rewards, and one of those rewards is an incredible fanbase that eagerly await each installment. Thank you for that.

Unfortunately, writing and releasing a book a month is not a pace I can continue. I am not a fast writer, nor do I use ghost writers or co-writers. I am not saying using those is wrong – all writers must find what works for them. I am a storyteller blessed with outstanding writing voices. I've found I require time outside the writing chair to keep me grounded mentally and keep the writing voices happy. The Jerry McNeal Series isn't ending, just changing a little – at least for now.

I'm pleased to tell you that my Jerry and Gunter voices are still here and still talking, and we are working to bring you MORE. Up next is a full-length Jerry McNeal novel.

*Spirit of Deadwood* will be offered as a larger 6x9 book in both hardbound and softcover options.

*Spirit of Deadwood* is the first full-length Jerry McNeal novel, which picks up shortly after where book twelve ends.

A fun-filled ghostly adventure with a hint of romance, *Spirit of Deadwood* is for those who dare to believe in the unbelievable.

The eBook is on preorder for April 19th.

Please follow me on Amazon.

And sign up for my newsletter for updates and information on new releases.

https://www.sherryaburton.com/

# About the Author

Sherry A. Burton writes in multiple genres and has won numerous awards for her books. Sherry's awards include the coveted Charles Loring Brace Award, for historical accuracy within her historical fiction series, The Orphan Train Saga. Sherry is a member of the National Orphan Train Society, presents lectures on the history of the orphan trains, and is listed on the NOTC Speaker's Bureau as an approved speaker.

Originally from Kentucky, Sherry and her Retired Navy Husband now call Michigan home. Sherry enjoys traveling and spending time with her husband of more than forty years.